The Jade Necklace

Original Title: The Jade Necklace (Symphony of Dusk #1)

©2015 Jad El Khoury

All rights reserved. No part of this publication may be reproduced, stored in or introduced into a retrieval system, or transmitted in any form or by any means, electronic, mechanical, photocopying, recording or otherwise without the prior written permission of the author.

First Edition 2016

ISBN 978-1523269815

http://www.tadrospublishing.com

Layout: Charbel Tadros

Cover Design: Abdallah Ghanem

Editing: Chris Khatschadourian, Joanne Chlela and Nadine Makarem

To my manager Georges Bou Mansour and his family, my students (you know who you are) from whom I've learned so much, my test reader (you won't be named but you've been awesome) and my mentor Nadia Tabbarra (Name spelled incorrectly).

Jad El Khoury

JAD EL KHOURY

Symphony of Dusk

Volume 1

The Jade Necklace

TADROS PUBLISHING

Acknowledgments

I would like to thank my editors: Joanne Chlela, Chris Khatschadourian and Nadine Makarem for their hard work, and our talented designer Abdalla Ghanim; as well as the team at Tadros Publishing and everyone who had been part of this project in one way or another.

I wish to thank everyone who has ever encouraged me: Miss Nayiri Babodjian, T.C.V.C.K.C, Dr.Vahid Behmardi, Cloe, Zoe and Latte, Layla and every single person who ever believed in me as a storyteller.

The Jade Necklace

Prologue: Hiding with the Monsters

Darkness and water had a common trait: she couldn't breathe in both of them. For that reason, when she closed the closet door, she kept a small crack open so that she wouldn't drown in obscurity. Outside, the birds were twittering, singing to one another about the sun and grass. But inside her cage, Clara – a six year old girl with olive-jade eyes, a small nose, and thin lips – could not find a reason to sing.

She peered through the slit. Beams of light and dancing fairies flooded the pink walled room and settled on her bed, the one with the mermaid covers. The white hinged door leading to the hallway was closed, but her enemy could creep in at any moment.

She was a princess now, no longer "daddy's little monkey". But there was no time to be happy about it because the witch was coming to get her. Clara had to remain in hiding, or else she would be caught and eaten. She quietly wrapped herself in a pink blanket. She waited.

The high heels clip-clopped first, then the smell of Chanel filled her tiny nostrils and Clara knew that the witch was near – the stronger the scent, the nearer the witch. In her tummy full of butterflies, she knew that sooner or later her hiding spot would be revealed.

Her tiny jade eyes peaked through the crack again and saw the witch stepping into the room. The witch made her way towards the bed and checked underneath it.

Why would I hide with the monsters? She thought. She would never, never-ever hide under the bed.

"Where *are* you, princess?" The witch called, singing the words, prolonging the 'are'. It was the classic Disney, high-pitched tone of a witch: sharp and out of tune. "You know I'll find you. I'll find you and I'll eat you, princess. Where *are* you?"

"You're never going to find me." Clara mumbled. But then, as the butterflies in her stomach started dancing, she thought: *I really hope not!*

The witch was a very beautiful woman. She had black hair at shoulder length and a small nose that resembled Clara's very much. Her olive-jade eyes were the same as Clara's, as were her thin, pink lips.

Clara was still peeping when the witch stood up and turned to look at the closet. Her lips curled into a wicked smile and the princess knew she was in trouble. Around the witch's neck hung a beautiful, jade stone necklace. "It must be the source of the witch's power," Clara thought, planning how she could steal it from her. The phone rang downstairs; if she could only get to it, someone would surely come for help.

The witch started towards the closet. Clara shut her eyes and covered her head with the pink blanket.

"Where are you, princess? Don't think you can hide from me." The witch was a mere step away from the hideout and the little princess was trapped.

"Found ya!" The witch jerked the closet door open as Clara leaped out of it like a rabbit. She grabbed the girl, still inside her shield of a blanket, and threw her on the bed. Clara freed her head from under the blanket just as she was attacked by ten fingers wiggling at her skin. She couldn't help but turn red with laughter.

"I'm going to eat you!" The witch said, now tickling the girl all over.

But Clara suddenly reached for the jade necklace and, with one quick motion, pulled it off her Mommy's neck. Game over.

"Clara!" Mommy scolded and stopped the tickling. *Being tickled is fun and giggly*; however, once it starts, there is nothing Clara wouldn't do to stop it. The worst part about playing make-believe was the witch's tickling. Still, she was sorry for pulling off Mommy's necklace. Mommy had had it around her neck for as long as she could remember.

"Why'd you do that baby?" Mommy asked, and Clara hid inside the cave that the blanket had formed.

"Clara – come out, sweetie."

But Clara was feeling too guilty to come out. So, Mommy pealed her out of the cavern and gave her a reassuring smile.

"I'm sorry." The little girl said, and handed Mommy the necklace. Mommy kissed Clara's forehead and then took the necklace and placed it in her own pocket.

"I want to go home. I don't like this vacation. There's no one to play with!" Clara complained.

Mommy took her in her arms and the girl laid her head on Mommy's pillow-like chest.

"Yara will be back soon. You girls can play together."

But Clara knew that her older sister would never play with her, especially now that she had made a friend, a *fat* friend, whom Clara despised.

"I want to go home," she cried. "Why can't we go back? I want to go home!"

"We're on vacation. We're here to have fun sweetie." Mommy put the girl down on the bed right next to the beautiful Ariel. It wasn't really the little mermaid, just a drawing of her; but that wouldn't stop them from being friends. "Tell you what," Mommy continued, "hmm... tomorrow, I'll take you to the beach!"

"They don't have a beach here"

"Well, the lake..." Mommy said with a most genuine smile.

But Clara wasn't satisfied. She knew something had to be wrong. They had left their home in such a rush after that strange man in black visited them. She didn't understand why they couldn't stay home and have daddy whip him with his belt if he had meant them any harm.

"I don't want the lake! I WANT TO GO HOME!" The princess shouted. She got off the bed and made her way to the small window overlooking the driveway.

Clara was raised in an upper-middle class family in San Francisco. She was the kind of child who was used to getting her way with both of her parents. From toys to books to candy, she had it all. But the one who was pampered the most was her older sister, Yara. Clara envied her for the freedom she had to visit friends and plan play dates. Still, that wasn't much of a problem. Back at home, life was as great as it could be.

In the mornings, Clara would wake up to the sound of an "Oops I did it again" alarm clock, force herself out of bed, as all children who love sleeping do, and then wash her face in a pink bathroom that she shared with her sister. Later, after choosing the prettiest dress to wear for the day, Mommy would fix her ponytail. Then she would join Daddy, Mommy, and Yara for breakfast – chocolate cereal and milk. She often heard her Mommy say that she ate too much for a six-year-old but her dad, the pediatrician, kept on reassuring her that Clara was growing and she needed all of the nourishment she could get.

After breakfast, Daddy would drop Clara off to school where she would brilliantly impress all of her favorite teachers. It was known that Clara was the ideal student and she liked it. Little did they know, however, that when no one was looking, she was a little devil.

When she was five, Clara had managed to learn how to read and this had shocked everyone – family, friends of family, teachers, and neighbors. She had heard that kids in general, Yara included, couldn't manage to read and write as well as she did before the third or fourth grade. Consequently, Clara, who loved impressing her family, developed a thirst for knowledge.

A few days before the start of the current school year, she had discovered the secret to human reproduction. For a whole weekend, she devotedly read about it, coming across a bunch of scary pictures in huge tomes she found on her father's bookshelves. She then took it upon herself to share her findings with a couple of her classmates by drawing the interlocking human bodies on a small copybook. The two girls she had decided to educate turned on her and threatened to deliver the copybook to the headmistress if she didn't give them her lunch money for the rest of the curriculum year. But Clara was not willing to give in to their threats. Instead, she herself headed to the principal's office and told him that those two girls stole her copybook and drew very disgusting "grown-up" things in it. The girls were expelled.

Like so many kids her age, Clara was afraid of the dark. That is why Mommy would always be there at bedtime to tell her a story. Clara's favorite was the

Tragedy of Princess Arisha. Mommy had once told her that the story was very real and that the book from which it had come from was long lost. She also said that perhaps, someday, someone would find it and uncover many truths about that old Kingdom. *The Book of the Dead* it was called and Clara wanted to be the one to find it.

Clara missed her home, especially her tree house where she and Crystal, her stuffed monkey, always had tea together. She missed her beautiful pink bed, her school, her teachers, and her friends. She still could not understand why her parents seemed so terrified after the man in black had visited them. Daddy, a strong man with big arms, could have easily taken him down without breaking a sweat. Why couldn't they go back home?

"Clara! Our lives do not revolve around you! We're staying here." Mother affirmed, almost yelling at her.

Clara, sad and let down, looked out the window at the clear blue sky as Mommy got off the bed. She would not cry but her eyes wallowed up in tears that were forbidden to stream down her cheeks. Sometimes she wished that she could fly. What if she were some Super girl who came from another planet? What if she were a girl with superpowers, meant to do great deeds? She would be able to visit heaven whenever she wanted and hug Baby Jesus. She could see Nana again. She could fight the fat girl and fly far away from her little cage. But a super girl can't fly when she's six years old just like little birds can't leave the nest before they can fly.

Mommy made her way across the room and went downstairs, leaving the door open. This was not really Clara's room and she hated it.

She despised the pink walls and more so the family photo from last Halloween that hung on the wall across from her bed. In it, she wore a beautiful wedding dress, whereas Yara was a cowgirl. If she can't go back home, why would she have to see constant reminders of a happier time?

On the ground underneath the portrait, her dollhouse rested. She, Yara, and daddy had made it themselves and it was the one thing she would never want to abandon. The dollhouse was more of a "doll mansion" actually; *a piece of home.*

By the window, opposite the door, there was a strange desk- that was also a series of book shelves. She hated that desk. The only fun aspect about the room, apart from the dollhouse, was the wall adjacent to it. It could change into the closet she hid in. *Back at home, we had a real closet.*

Still, at least she had her own room. Yara had another room, but whenever she was scared at night, she would go sleep next to her. Yara had big bones and could hit the monsters that come from under the bed. Besides, she was nine. No one knew that Clara was afraid of the monsters, so why could she not go outside whenever she wanted, just like Yara?

Clara stood by the window and basked. The beam of fairies seemed to dance all around her. Birds pecked at the green lawn around the trunk of the Platanus tree, then took to the blue skies. It was then that a black car parked in the driveway just as Mommy came back in with a Kinder surprise.

"Why can Yara go out whenever she wants and I can't? I'm six!"

The Jade Necklace

"Because you're my little Princess." Mommy handed Clara the chocolate bar and as she unwrapped it, peering out the window, she saw three men step out of the car and head towards their front door.

"A princess can go wherever she wants!"

"Very well; does her highness wish to hear a story?"

"Yes, please," replied Clara when they heard a knock on the door.

The door downstairs opened. She heard glass shattering and men grunting. Her daddy started to shout. Clara ran towards her bedroom door but Mommy yanked her off her feet and placed her behind her. She then shut the door. They heard more sounds of crashing and fighting coming from below and Clara began to cry. She couldn't understand what was happening. Was someone hurting her daddy? *Do the bad men want to kidnap me? Is the man in black here to hurt us?*

"Mommy, what's happening?"

"Get under the bed." Mommy urged.

"No."

"Do as I say. Now!"

The monsters can't hurt me if mommy is here.

Clara crawled under the bed and laid there quietly. She could see Mommy's feet stand firmly in front of the door. *She'll protect me.* This wasn't the first time someone had come for them. *The man in black couldn't hurt us before.* She put her hand in her pocket and felt something solid in there. She took it out and found Mommy's jade necklace. She swiftly tucked it back in, failing to understand how it found its way into her possession. The door opened and a man's boots hastily stepped into the room. He shut the door behind him. *Daddy!*

"He's here?" asked Mommy.

"No," replied Daddy.

It was in that moment that the door blew open and several black shoes stepped in. The little princess realized that living an adventure is scarier than watching one on television. She did not want to be a Super Girl anymore. She just wanted to be Clara.

She could tell from the way their feet danced on the tiles, that the intruders were fighting Mommy and Daddy. *Daddy can kick your butts.* Deep down, she was worried though. What would happen if Mommy and Daddy lost? What will the bad guys do to the little princess, should they prevail?

"You can't have her!" Mommy yelled when two of the intruders fell to the ground. They seemed to look like regular men. They were really big, relative to Clara, but were much smaller than daddy, less muscular and evidently weaker! One of the men instantly stood up while the other caught her with his eye. He spotted her under the bed and she realized that he might not be completely human, for there was something strange about his eyes: they were yellow with oval pupils like a cat's. He crawled towards her hastily but Mommy's hands managed to snap his neck and he fell lifeless on the floor beside the bed.

"Where is she?" said one man with a hoarse voice when Clara noticed that one of the other men had caught on fire and was moving madly around the room. *Where did the fire come from?*

"Or what?" replied Mommy in a glacial tone.

"What are you doing?" yelled Daddy.

"We can't let them find her." Mommy said.

The burning man flailed about and made the whole room catch on fire. Her beautiful doll house was burning: all the dolls, the furniture, the beautiful dining room that she and Yara had designed.... *Is our own house going to burn down too?* Mommy and Daddy stood still facing the intruders. Neither of them moved or spoke. *Were they frozen?*

Were they afraid of the fire? Black smoke slowly filled the air and Clara began to cough. Her eyes grew watery. She could not see. She could not tell if Mommy and Daddy were still there. *Am I alone in the burning room?* It didn't matter. She knew she could not escape. She could not breathe, she was submerged in darkness. *Mommy said to stay here. I will stay under the bed. They will save me! Mommy and Daddy will save me!* The last thing her olive-jade eyes saw was the gloomy wings of death. Then, it was all dark and she was hiding with the monsters.

The Jade Necklace

Chapter One: Prowler

It was one of the darkest autumn nights, for neither the moon nor the stars dared shine upon the earth. The streets were silent and the skies empty. Empty, that is, if it weren't for a bat-like creature that had taken flight. It was soaring high into the night sky. Its skin was hard and of the same complexion as its shady surroundings.

The creature was on the hunt, prowling. It required nourishment to remain strong and be able to face its enemies that could be trying to hunt it still. No one could blame it for it had to eat.

London had been its home for a while now and it liked it. It had all the food it could sink its fangs into, free of charge. The London Eye showed from a distance and it grinned knowing that no matter how high the humans reached they could never truly be as powerful and all knowing. Higher and higher it went into the sky until the tall buildings were nothing but tiny dots on a map with the river Thames coursing midway between them. The creature dove down into a residential area far from the larger than life buildings.

It sniffed its prey down in an alley. It landed on the roof top of one of the many nightclubs with a thud, its hind-claws digging deep into the granite roof. It made its way to the edge and examined the surroundings with its red eyes that could instill fear in anyone's heart. It needed to find a prey that was suitable for its taste. Its gaze caught two shadowy figures in the alley behind the club. The loud music echoed in the night, but its senses were beyond a mere human's and it could clearly hear the pleas of a prospective victim down there.

A man in a black coat held a young boy at gun point and asked for his money. The creature chuckled cheekily for it had found its prey. The man with the gun took the other one's belongings and set off into the night. The thief could sense that he was being watched. The creature smelled his fear. The man tried to pick up his pace to escape whatever it was that was watching him.

The creature growled, spread its large black wings that were double the size of its muscular and large body and swooped in from the sky. The man looked back and saw a 2.5 meter long winged devil about to pierce him with its claws. It was then that he tripped and, falling, tried to shoot at it only to find that the bullets did not hit the target. The winged devil had maneuvered itself out of their trajectory with ease. The man quickly rolled to the side as the creature attempted to land on top of him, stood up and ran only to be pushed down from behind. He got up a second time but the creatures' hind paws gave him a kick. He was on the ground again. It grabbed him by his legs and flew into the sky with the man wailing and screaming as he dangled upside down. The creature's long black scaly tail wrapped itself around his mouth, silencing him.

The smell of fear was intoxicating. It made the creature hungry and it greatly craved the taste of the flesh it was about to devour. After mere seconds, the creature let go of the man and he fell, crashing down onto a rooftop. It then landed in front of him with a thud. The creature whipped its tail as it started towards the shivering, barely conscious thug. Its face was calm and peaceful and did not show any form of emotion. It had a square-like head that was double the size of a normal man's. As it approached the retreating prey, it opened its jaw and growled as though it were a lion guarding its territory. It was then that the man saw the long canines: unlike a normal human, it had four upper and four lower canines as sharp as steak knives.

"What do you want with me?" pleaded the man as he retracted into a corner.

The ground seemed to shake beneath the creature's paws and the man cried out for help. Before he could scream for help, the creature had ripped his carotid apart with its fore-claws. Thick blood splattered across the creature's face and on the walls. It gushed out of the man's neck in a pulsatile fashion that was synchronized to his decelerating heartbeat. As the prey fell to the floor, the fountain that had formed at his neck continued to eject the viscous red which dribbled to his sides and onto the ground. The creature then sunk its teeth into his belly devouring muscle and entrails alike. It ate until there was nothing left of the man, not even his bones. Nothing, except for the red that had colored its lips, face, hands and torso. It was as if it had bathed in the man's blood. The creature took flight again. It was several minutes until it flew over an Olympic pool that was situated in the backyard of a large mansion. It landed on the front porch just as dawn announced itself. The first rays of a red sun warmed the marble terrace, which was surrounded from both sides by a green grass.

As it breathed in the light of dawn, its hind claws withdrew into its skin, just as its legs took on a white complexion and became those of an athletic human being's. Its torso was no longer black but white revealing a magnificent muscular form. A tattoo that spelled his name in Arabic was found on his shoulder: بدر. His face was no longer square and beastly but handsome. The man had long black curly hair, a curved nasal ridge, and hazel eyes instead of red. He truly was a marvel to the eye and, more importantly, he was well aware of it. As a beast, he could catch any prey he wanted to feed upon; as a man, he could get anyone he wanted into his bed.

Bader walked towards his mansion's front door and went up the cold marble steps to find the house key under a black mat. He unlocked the door and stepped in. The large iron-gate behind him was still locked. It served as a main entrance to his mansion but he had never resorted to it in the early mornings anyway since he'd always flew right above it and swooped in, courtesy of his wings. He stepped inside then looked out one of the small glass windows that had been incorporated into his large door. He saw that the sun had taken on its usual yellow tint. A new day had come and he wasn't about to remain cooped up until the sun goes down. The likes of him did not need sleep. He could sleep at night if he wanted to and that would prevent him from turning but he loved to glide upon the wing, to grind the bones of villains with his molars. He worshipped the way blood rolled over his tongue warming it with its complex texture. He could prevent himself from turning at night, if he wanted to, for all the sustenance he'd need he could get in human form. He could prevent himself from turning by sleeping in at night or by remaining calm and attuned to his inner goodness. But he did not want to! He chose to turn every night and he was satisfied.

It was still too early in the morning. He decided to hit his very own indoor gym in nothing but boxer shorts. Few people had a full floor of their home structured into a full-fledged gym and he was one of the lucky few. It had every type of equipment any man would dream of, as well as a shower and a sauna! He first hopped onto the treadmill for about thirty minutes, and then began his daily Hulk-style exercise of one hour till the sweat made his flexed muscles more defined than they actually were. Each muscle was drawn on his body with utter perfection and he believed that was why he could fuck someone every night. Every woman wanted him behind her, inside of her. Every girl wanted to be held down and pounded by someone like him and he knew it. He felt himself stiffen, took off his shorts and trotted into the shower. Human flesh was an aphrodisiac, he thought, as his cock hardened. He was more hung than an average male, something he took pride in. He never laid a hand on it for he believed that as long as one can fuck a real person, why waste time with a lesser pleasure?

When he had finished his cold shower, his hardness had also passed. He put on a towel and walked back into the training space, grabbed his cellphone and dialed a number.

"Good morning Reed." He spoke, sitting on a bench.

"Good morning, I..."

"I heard that you were planning a merger. Why didn't I hear of that?"

"You were having dinner... It's a good idea, you know. If you could let me explain and..."

"Your father was a good man. I would hate it if something bad were to happen to his son .You will not go on with the merger, Reed. Am I clear?"

"But the economy... Bader, I..."

"Reed, don't make me repeat myself."

"I know, I understand. I'll figure something out..."

"You know I trust you Reed; otherwise, I wouldn't have left you in charge. Handle it."

"I will. Are we still on for that dinner? Sera wanted me to check with you."

"Tell her I'm looking forward to try her cooking."

"I still didn't tell her about…"

He hung up.

Bader had worked with Marcus Reed's family for generations and trusted them to keep his identity secret for centuries. He made them what they were, he helped them attain power and wealth, and in return they were his connection to the human world. Bader "Jacobs" owned a company, the main aspect of which was an auction house that was supposedly passed down to him through fictional generations. Reed and the company were based in Paris and he flew there on the "Bader express". He did not like the words: Bader express, but somehow the silly nickname Reed used to refer to his winged form had nested in his mind. *Who knew geek as a state of being was contagious.* In Paris, under the guise of Mr. Jacobs, he was treated like royalty by all the employees and more than once contemplated feeding on those that were embezzling. He was the owner and his ancestor the founder, but the CEO was Marcus Reed and his father before him.

Bader stepped out of his mansion in a tight red shirt that highlighted the firmness of his large pecks and gave a hint to the eight packs that were his abs. He put on an expensive silver earing and black jeans that assembled his crotch into what seemed to be a gigantic flaccid bolus waiting to be pleasured, leaving no room for imagination as to how big it would be once fully hard. He strode with confidence along the bustling streets, for he was on the hunt again.

It hadn't been long since he moved to London, but he had grown fond of it. He had quickly learned that in this city, everything that he could want was within his grasp. When hungry, he could dine in the best of restaurants or on the finest human flesh. Once hard, he could fuck whoever he wanted. However, that had been the case of every city he'd lived in until he grew tired of it, the city that is, not the lifestyle, never the lifestyle.

As he walked, he couldn't help but notice a fine woman walking beside him. The first things he saw were her firm and plump tits. She had long auburn hair that he could pull when he'd ride her and a curvy fit ass that he'd want to ravish incessantly. She strolled slowly along the street carrying nothing but a small black bag. He decided to follow. She seemed to walk to the rhythm of an oriental tune which reminded him of a belly dancer that he had bonked some fifty years ago.

The auburn haired beauty ventured into Hyde Park, and he decided to follow inconspicuously. She quietly headed towards a bench, took a seat and began reading a novel that she pulled out of her bag. At least he'd be fucking someone with brains, he thought. In the blink of an eye, he was next to her. In his beast form, he could move faster than sound, and in his human form in spite of the limitations he could still walk faster than any man, run faster than an Olympic champion and lift double what any heavy weight champion could with ease.

"Interesting book you got there." He pointed out as he stood in the shade of a thick branched tree.

"You know what they say. All of the handsome ones are gay." She teased. His pupils found hers and noticed that they were dilated. That could only mean one thing: she's interested or intrigued.

"Finding twilight interesting does not make a man gay." He lies. *Twilight is the most disgusting chick-flick book ever made.*

"Please, spare me..." She continued to tease as his eyes floated off for an instant to watch a running squirrel make its way to the top of a tree. Aurora had been his own squirrel all those years ago, but all he had left of her were the bitter memories of the day that *he* took her from him.

"Would you like some proof?" He pushed all thoughts of Aurora to the back of his mind and focused on the tail he was trying to chase.

"Why doesn't Edward want to turn Bella into a vampire?"

"Because ... that's what he wants..."

"So you haven't read it."

"Not a chance... How many times have you read it anyway?"

"Third time and counting"

She tugged a curl behind her right ear and he smiled.

"I can show you that I'm as straight as they come. My place is a few minutes away."

She hesitated but he knew he had her then and there. This was getting too easy for him. He would put on that smile of his, look them straight in the eyes, assert his self-confidence with his tone, and let his body language fueled with desire and self-esteem do the rest.

"Let's see what you can do"

He extended his arm and she took it. They walked silently towards his apartment, neither attempting to break the silence. This was no easy prey. She, very much like him, was a hunter, he thought. That or she was just a cock hungry bitch who needed her daily dose of dick.

When they reached the apartment, she walked straight into the bedroom, slipped into comfortable nudity and lay on the bed.

"I thought we'd skip the small talk."

He took off his shirt revealing his muscular body and sensed her whole body shivering from afar. He unhurriedly approached and ran his hand through her hair. Her luscious pink lips found his index finger and suckled on it like a lollipop. He smiled at her, and she laughed gleefully.

"What will the gay boy do to me now?" she teased, as his fingers found her wetness. She stood up to kiss him, their tongues interlocking as three of his fingers throbbed inside of her. He carried her off the bed, her legs encircling his thighs. He glued her body on to his, hard enough so she could feel the erection.

"I want you," she said as she savagely bit his lips. He placed her back onto the King sized Venetian bed. As soon as he had her there, her hands found a way to unbutton his trousers. She rolled to her side as he positioned himself behind her. He placed one of her legs on his and slowly slid inside of her. His movement began to quicken, however, in synchrony with her loud moans. It was then that she lay on her stomach for her leg had spasmed and he knew that it had tired but he had not. He kept on pounding her while pulling on to her hair, pulling harder and harder as she screamed in ecstasy dumbing down the squeaking of the bed beneath them.

He flipped her onto her back while still inside her and kept on giving it to her as her hands found their way to his buttock pulling him further in. She bid him to quicken his motion with her hands. He pulled himself to his knees and his cock almost slid out of her. She held onto to his back and, with one quick motion, sat on his dick taking every last centimeter of his hung cock. After letting her ride him for a while, he held on to her tightly and stood up by the bed, bent his knees slightly as if he were about to perform squats and pummeled her. Her entire weight rested on his cock and thighs but he was more than a match for the task. He was a real man and by the looks of it, she'd never been fucked by a real man before. As his cock slid in and out of her wet hole that ached he moved towards the dresser. He put her on there and checked out the scene in the mirror. He flexed his pecks for her and her body responded by tightening the grip around his dick to the point that he would have almost cum if he did not slow down. His right hand found its way to her breast and as he pinched the nipple of her left one, the right nipple rolled over his tongue. Her moans were more than he could handle. He was close and couldn't keep it up much longer. He plowed at her as hard and fast as he could and it seemed for moment that the friction of his junk against her loins would set them both on fire. He did not stop until they both reached an explosive rapture.

After the storm, he found the notion that she did not want to cuddle quite strange. She instantly got off the dresser and headed towards the shower. He attempted to join her but found that she had locked the door. This woman had somehow immediately understood his needs. He had no desire to form some "healthy" bond with another human being. People were there in his life for three reasons only: increase his wealth, spread their legs and bend over for him, and nourish him when needed. Oddly enough, he felt like taking her again but he put on his boxers and waited for her to come out.

She walked out of the shower naked, dripping water all over his cork flooring.

"There was no towel."

"Remind me to kill the cleaning lady." He pointed to the drawer.

"You would, wouldn't you?" she asked as she took a towel from the drawer and dried herself.

"I'm Bader Jacobs, by the way." Giving his name might incite her to let him ride her wet tightness again.

"Darla Potter." She replied as she put on her dress and shoes

He paced towards her and held her in his arms, his crotch already hardening again against her behind, and his hand slipping under her dress to cup her breast. But in that moment, she gasped for air and swiftly moved away from him. She breathed heavily for a moment and he could not comprehend what had come over her. She looked at him as if she beheld a monster and he immediately understood.

"I … I have to go." He did not answer, but merely fixated on her with his icy stare. She took a few steps back nervously. She grabbed her purse and headed for the door.

"Is something wrong?"

"No…" she smiled nervously. He tried to touch her hand but she instantly pulled away.

Anyone could have concluded by then that she had the *power of sight.* She obviously saw what he was. She was one of the rare people that could. *It's a good thing, they can't control when they get their visions. Can't imagine her bending over for me had she seen what I am before we got here.* He never understood what triggered the visions in a seer nor care.

"You know, don't you?" he asked quietly as she backed into a corner, her back against his black dresser. He could see himself approaching her in the mirror and knew that he looked terrifying.

 It was truly a rare gift, the sight, but by no means accompanied by other gifts. Those gifted with the sight had no active powers, nor special abilities. They could play neither the offensive nor the defensive. This girl had made a mistake in revealing what she knew of him, he could easily dispose of her. He wished she had kept her vision to herself but he had to do something.

"Kidding, can we fuck again?" He teased, hoping she would believe herself to be wrong. He did not wish to kill so early in the day, but would not hesitate to do so if he had to.

"You're a monster." She said as he found himself flung into the wall and crashing into Hokusai's "The Dream of the Fisherman's Wife" that hung above the bed.

"You're not just a seer, are you?" He asked once he was on his feet again next to the ruined original. This was a fair fight now, he thought. He knew now that the girl was telekinetic as well; a gift never found in a seer. He knew all too well that human seers could never be telekinetic, nor have any active powers. Perhaps this girl was no human after all.

He leaped towards her and punched her in the face. She fell to the ground with a bleeding nose. Bader saw her forming a fire ball in the palm of her hand and, before he could react, he was hit by it in the shoulder. Blood oozed from the black scar tissue it left behind. *Fire starter and telekinetic? No wonder she was a great fuck.*

He tried to regain his balance but she was onto him now. She kicked him in the crotch which hurt like a thousand and one hells then she telekinetically used him to smash the window. Shards of glass pierced his bloodied and bruised body. *I'm pissed.*

Darla started for the door. He sprung to his feet and, as quick as sound, rushed towards her, plunging a thick flake of glass into her back, damaging his own palm in the process. With a back kick, she threw him off of her long enough for her to remove the glass.

However, in a flash, his fist met her face several times till she fell to the ground with a bloodied nose and a bruised lip. With whatever strength she had left she lifted the bed with her mind so it would crash on to him. She had been unsuccessful. First crawling, then running, she headed for the door.

Blood and Fear. He felt like a predator once again. He felt as he had when he tore that man apart the night before, and he wanted nothing more but to sink his teeth into Darla's flesh. He knew she wouldn't go down without a fight, though. Their eyes interlocked. He sped towards her hoping to finish her off. She dodged him and punched him hard on the windpipe. He fell to the ground. He was incapacitated as he watched her hover over him.

"Wh...What are you?" he managed to ask with great effort, but she did not answer. This was no ordinary girl, of that he was sure. She was different from any human or mage he had ever encountered during his long years. *What are you?*

He knew that she could have aimed for the kill then and there but didn't. Her eyes spoke of hesitation. The girl was innocent of blood. He could finally move, and when he did, he used his leg to trip her and as she fell to the ground, he grabbed her by the neck.

"Game over," he whispered as his fist tightened around her neck.

Her cellphone began to ring.

The Jade Necklace

Chapter Two: Monster

One blow and the punching bag was freed of its chains and thrown across the room, landing on the trampoline. Bader was stronger than any man but he had to be careful now. He needed a new punching bag in the gym. He could always bring home a couple of thugs, tie them up and practice on them. He had to be cautious now in light of what had happened the previous day, especially during the hunts.

He had her pinned to the bedroom's parquet floor. Snapping her neck like a twig would have been easy for a man like him.

Alive, she would be a threat to him. She knew what he was and wanted him dead. The wise choice would have been to just snap her neck and be done with it –

but he did not. Her phone rang. The image of a teenage girl smiled at him from the screen. "Sis" it said. The younger girl was a blonde whose breasts had barely budded. *They must be close.*

He pulled away from her. She sprung to her feet and took on a defensive stance at first. The blood trickled from her nose, covering her mouth and chin. Her lower lip shook with vigor and he knew that she feared him. She picked up her phone which had stopped ringing and placed it in her pocket. Her eyes did not leave him and he knew she could strike again at any moment at her own peril. He asked her to leave but she only inched away keeping her guard up. He recognized that that was the natural defense mechanism but still he growled at her "NOW!"

He made a mistake when he underestimated her. She was strong, fast, and had many supernatural abilities. Who knows what other powerful friends she might have? Darla may still want him dead; he was a monster, after all. If that were her wish, then she would be striking again soon. She could make him pay for the mercy he had shown her. What was Darla though? He could clearly remember the pages of the *Book of*

Shadows that was owned by a powerful being he once knew: Mama Jinguala. She was an old woman with white hair, a crooked nose, and blackened teeth. A very distinctive giant black mole dwelled on her right cheek. Bader clearly remembered what she had taught him about mages, magical beings that were all too human if not for their powers, so that he would know what to expect on his hunts.

She had told him that not all humans were what they seemed. Some were born as mages and mages were special and powerful. He remembered that whenever a mage is born, he or she is born to an element. That personal symbol is not apparent to the naked eye but is metaphysical in nature. There are four of these elements and only a minuscule minority of mages discover what they are, let alone fulfill their true potential. One thing was for certain though: being a mage is something that is generally passed on through the generations from parent to child, though at times, it might skip a generation.

According to the *Book of Shadows* the four symbols were Earth, Fire, Water and Wind. Those who bear the element of earth made up 99% of the earth's mage population. They did not possess any special abilities by birth but were considered magical witches for they could cast spells and had the potential to grow very powerful if instructed properly. He recalled that there were seven levels to witchcraft and only those with the earth element can access true magic and rise through its levels. However, the last time people managed to rise to a level above the third was in ancient Greece, Phoenicia and Egypt, where many men and women advanced through the levels and came to be known as Gods.

Those born to the element of water possessed defensive powers. Each individual usually has one active power but some rare cases go on to develop many. Some of the abilities that these persons may have include: invincibility, healing powers, shape shifting and phasing, among other things.

As for Fire, its bearer possesses one or more offensive abilities such as strength, speed, telekinesis, teleportation, fire manipulation, electricity, and thunder strikes.

Last but not least, a person born to the element of Wind has the powers of sight. They may foresee the future and dream walk into one's mind. The strongest amongst them are able to channel other people's abilities as their own when in close proximity.

He distinctly remembered asking whether one mage could somehow bear more than one symbol.

A mage cannot belong to more than one element and no one element may overlap with another. So what was Darla? She had the sight possessed by wind and the strength possessed by fire. Was she a monster too? Or was she demonic? It could be possible that breeds of demons might have harvested the power of several mages and claimed them for their own. Darla could have been demon. But no! He would have sensed it, and she smelled human all right – at least, as human as a mage could get.

He was not much of a thinker and did not want to trouble himself with unnecessary concern. He hopped on the treadmill and ran at a rather humanly impossible speed until the stench of sweat had taken ahold of his nostrils. He decided to shower. If she were going to come back in full force, she would have already. He made his way to his bedroom, took off his clothes and walked into the master bathroom. He did not want to shower downstairs that day for he had been underground for too long. He stood motionless under the burning water. He had taken many lives before, fed on thousands of men. He ripped through their flesh and viscera. Yet, he let the girl go. Monstrosity aside, Bader had never taken an innocent life. Those he had maimed and killed were criminals, murderers, rapists... The girl, he believed, was innocent.

When she attacked him, she thought she was attacking a soulless beast. Then again, who wouldn't have thought that? He was a gargoyle, after all.

Gargoyles were fearsome creatures that once terrorized the world of men as they rampaged through livestock and humanity alike. The ruthless gargoyle leader, Caleb, had once been the bane of the dark ages as he scavenged castles and sheds to feed upon human flesh. For Caleb, humanity merely served two purposes: sustenance and sex. Rumors had it that he would rape any maiden of noble blood in front of her kin. Her body would break due to anatomical incompatibilities. It was rumored that the screams and pleas of the fathers would give him great ecstasy. Then, once he had had his pleasure, he would rip her to pieces and feast on her right before slaughtering everyone she had ever known. One could chalk it all up to rumors but Bader had a first-hand experience with the terror that was Caleb, Lord of the Gargoyles.

Immortal as they may be, the gargoyles had one weakness: daylight was their curse. For when the sun shined upon the earth, they slumbered in stone. It was that intrinsic weakness that had most probably brought about their extinction. If it weren't for daylight, they could have bred until their population exceeded that of the humans and a new world order could have been established. Those troubles were over a thousand years ago and there was no point to dwelling in the past. The silver lining: gargoyles stopped aging when they reached adulthood but they could breed indefinitely over the course of their immortal lives.

After he was dressed and set to go for his daily walk, there was a banging on the door and then silence. He reached the entrance when the door burst open.

He stood still for a moment and in that split second several men barged in. Bader found himself flying across the hallway and pinned against the living room wall. *Telekinesis!* One of the men, tall and fit, gave him an empty stare. Bader then found himself floating in mid air while flames burned in the atmosphere around him. He floated amid a sphere of fire that consumed all oxygen from his vicinity and he could no longer breathe.

"Jacob, we want him alive." An older balding man with green eyes commanded.

"Don't worry, Georges. This won't kill him." Said a cocky young man who couldn't be older than twenty.

Oxygen grew scarce and Bader began to cough. He attempted to punch his way through the fire but burned his hand. His scream seemed to bounce off the fiery walls surrounding him and strike at his ears with full force, almost piercing his ear drums. The surroundings dimmed and consciousness was snuffed out of him. He floated into the ether, into darkness.

"Robin, Robin," she called out to him in his half sleep. It couldn't be her. He began to remember the agonizing fire, suffocating, the burns... It must have consumed him whole. He was dead.

No, that couldn't be right. If he were dead, then seeing her would mean that she had gone to hell as well. She was beautiful, innocent and pure; a fair maiden like her could not belong with him in the afterlife. She should have gone to heaven! He who had killed dozens did not deserve to meet her again upon death.

"Robin, my love..."

It was her voice again, in the darkness. Was this his punishment? She was as fleeting as a breeze under a scorching sun. It was torture to feel her presence but unable to touch her soft skin nor smell her soft golden hair, to forever yearn for her loving smile which was hard enough without adding her voice to the equation. Was it his punishment to never again bask in those jade eyes knowing that they are so close?

A smooth, minuscule hand touched his face and he knew it was hers. He had not forgotten the feel of the one he had loved long ago when he was more man than beast.

"Open your eyes." He felt her warm breath on his ear sending a jolt through every fiber of his body.

I can't. Even if his eyes *were* open, he would be too blinded to see her. The fates would never grant him release and his release was in her alone. If he were to open his hazel eyes, she would be gone again. He was either dead or hallucinating, but, either way, he did not want to move past his current state.

He breathed in the darkness that surrounded him. It filled his lungs with an agony that he had never known but he endured. *I miss you.*

"Together forever, remember?"

The gloom began to slowly fade. He caught a glimpse of her golden locks gliding on the soft breeze. He could not make out her features for the light that emanated from her was too bright. He wanted nothing more than to slip his fingers through those beautiful golden strands. He wished to take her in his embrace and let her sleep upon his chest as she used to in a time long forgotten. The light that shone off of her began to fade and he could clearly see her standing before him. They were not in a physical space. They floated in darkness but he didn't care. She wore a white gown that befit a lady of her class. But, most importantly, she still wore upon her neck the jade necklace she had once asked him to keep safe. She was more beautiful than ever and he was ready to give his life if it meant he could kiss her thin red lips again and drown in her olive-jade eyes.

"Aurora... I..." He awoke abruptly as a searing pain overtook his serenity.

The Jade Necklace

Jad El Khoury

Chapter Three: A Day in Clara's Life

The house was on fire. She looked up at it from the garden. The fire did not prevent her from racing towards it. She strode on the yellowed grass, with tears in her eyes, hoping against hope that she would make it this time.

She reached for the door, but every time she walked through it, she found herself right where she started. Her parents were in there; she needed to save them at all cost.

It was time to fly; she levitated and reached the window to see her burning parents. *The screams, o my god, the screams – fire consumes everything, the good and the bad alike, the cowardly and the brave.* Everything burned: the closet, the bed, the dollhouse. And when the screams stopped, she could no longer tell the difference between her charcoaled mother and father. She cried out, unable to get in and save them.

She felt sharp things pierce into her shoulders and was lifted higher into the night sky. She suffered from the creature's claws as they punctured deeper into her skin. She looked up to see two flaming eyes, eyes she would never forget.

And the devil saved me from the fire.

The creature suddenly let go of her and she spiraled towards the ground. Fear had no place in her heart. Fear had nothing on those who had nothing to lose. She would land safely, as always. A French song played far in the background. Before she reached the ground, she realized that the song was sung by Lara Fabian, her roommate's favorite musician. *The dream is over.* Morning had come, and she willed herself to consciousness.

****

It was seven in the morning when Clara woke up. Her alarm hadn't gone off yet and she was forced to open her eyes on the account of this annoying brat's self-centeredness.

The room was messy, as messy as her roommate. An open yet empty pizza box lay on the floor by the other bed. An entire closet's worth of dirty clothes was piled on their study desk, and the one comfortable chair was buried in Carmen's red and black lingerie. Carmen was still in her underwear as she slow danced to her annoying French music. There was no point in hoping that she would turn it down anytime soon. *Tango mi amor, l'un de nous est plus fort, just shut that music and let me sleep, Tango mi amor!*

"Good morning princess," Carmen said enthusiastically as she raised the volume to Clara's inconvenience.

Still dancing, Carmen put on a micro black skirt that kept her killer legs on display. Clara couldn't understand how that girl's brain functioned: *two thirds of the campus population visit what's under that skirt more than they visit the library.* The answer was simple.

Carmen tried to get by in life with what she had on the outside, because she knew she lacked what she needed on the inside. She had amazing bronze skin tone, long black locks that dangled around her shoulders, and hazel eyes that most men would get lost in. Yet again, Clara thought, God gives from one side and takes from the other – or so they say in Lebanon.

"Could you please lower the…" Clara muttered but as usual Carmen did not let her complete the sentence and interrupted with her typical 'friendly' chatter.

"Hey listen, there's this party tonight, and I think it would be awesome if you could show up. We'd be the hottest girls there. How about it?" she said, her eyes glowing. Clara tried to wrap her mind around how that creature could not sense the utter resentment she felt towards her.

"I'll let you know, I guess," said Clara as she sat up in bed.

"No, princess, 'maybe' won't do. You have to come. Do you know how many hot guys will be there? I mean look at you, if I were a lesbian I'd so go out with you. Those boys will drool when they see you," Carmen argued.

Clara fought the urge to punch her in the face. She couldn't help but wonder about her sister, Yara; had she survived the attack, would she have grown up to become as annoying as this Carmen? Clara never got along with Yara and this exact scenario would have been very plausible. But she didn't want to think of the dead. Life is for the living; life is here and now.

"I don't really care about hot boys at some party," Clara explained, her mind drifting back to the night of the fire. *Yara wasn't around the house or anywhere close so why was she never found? And that winged creature, I must have dreamt it.* But who saved her from the burning house in Geneva and brought her to an orphanage in Beirut? All she could recall was a monstrous creature smashing in the windows then pulling her from under the bed. With her in its clawed arms, it flew out the window into the night sky for what seemed to be forever. She remembered having screamed and screamed until she fainted and when she eventually came to she was in another country, another city and could not speak the language. *It was the smoke, I must have hallucinated.* When she later asked about her parents, no records were found of them or of

Yara. It was as though her family never existed, as though she did not exist before the fire. There was no record of Clara having ever existed and the psychiatrist thought that the poor street girl must have been too traumatized to remember her real life, so she concocted a fantasy world.

When the Kfouries adopted her, they still called her Clara and loved her as if she were their own daughter but they did not tolerate any mention of her imaginary past. With time, Clara learned to stop talking about it. But she never forgot. As an adult, she tried to dig deeper into the history of the house but could find nothing. She tried to find any semblance of information about her life in San Francisco but there was nothing to find as well. For all intents and purposes, the Clara that she was and her family had never existed.

Her stream of thought was interrupted by Carmen's soprano.

"Fine, forget about the boys. We'll have fun together; we'll dance and go crazy. Come on, princess, it'll be fun." She plead as if she were an ugly little baby. Clara got out of bed and looked into the mirror that stood erect on a commode by the door, next to their desk. *A desk that was also a bookcase, just like in Geneva.* She looked at her long, dark hair that fell onto her shoulders, her petite ruby lips, tiny straight nose, and pink skin that covered her nimble form.

Her hand went straight to her mother's jade necklace and, as she held it in her hand, she could feel a sorrow wash over her. The necklace went perfectly well with her jade eyes but that wasn't why she wore it. She wore it always. It was a piece of home, the only proof she wasn't seeing things, never imagined things. The man in black was real and he will come for her one day even if no one believed her.

"I'll talk it over with Andrew and the others; if they want to come I don't see why not." Clara replied, hoping to end the conversation then and there.

"Fine... don't think I'll be dropping the subject, princess." She replied before turning off the stereo and heading to the restroom. *Peace, at last.*

*****

A few hours later, Clara sat with her friends, Andrew and Widad, in the cafeteria for their usual lunch gathering. The two were already seated at a table by the window that overlooked a green field known as 'The Green Field'.

"Hey, Clara," Widad greeted her adorably as Clara approached. She wore a shirt with bunnies sown into the fabric; it made Clara smile a little. Widad was a 'well-rounded' girl - fat was an understatement. She had red hair and she was half French, which made her a plump, Irish looking Lebanese with a French accent. She had cute freckles that covered her face and sea blue eyes, filled with innocence.

"Hey sweetie. Hi Andy." Clara joined them.

Andrew smiled and nodded. Andrew was of small stature, dirty blond, with brown eyes. He was what Clara would describe as fit but with tiny muscles. And observing his behavior, she could also deduce that Andrew was "still in the closet."

"Where's Erick?" She asked, the answer already known to her.

"Getting Grace-Marie from her class. You know how the poor thing can't walk the lonely halls on her own," joked Andrew to Clara's comfort. She wasn't the only one who found Grace-Marie to be completely inappropriate for Erick. Erick was a charming, black-haired Adonis. His eyes were of a strange darkness that moved every fiber inside of her. His nose had the most perfect of imperfections for in spite of its quasi-large size, it ornamented his face ideally. His body was sculptured like a Greek god – the male equivalent of Aphrodite, she believed. He had broad shoulders, large firm pecks, washboard abs, and a back that redefined her fetish for muscular male backs. Grace-Marie, on the other hand, was a petite fake blonde with green eyes, her nose the product of many botched plastic surgeries, her lips blood red, probably due to her vampirism. *Yes, she's definitely a vampire and she's got him under her thrall.* Grace-Marie's body was not as fit as Clara's but the girl claimed to be on a constant diet and did go on rare jogs whenever she managed not to misplace her iPod. However, Clara couldn't for the life of her understand what Erick saw in that girl. Clara suddenly held on to her green necklace and felt heat emanate from it. Perhaps, she had been right all along and the necklace had an innate power to it. Or, perhaps, it's just her anger and sweaty palms caused by the subject at hand.

"They're back together?" Clara asked trying to make the question sound as casual as she could. She sometimes wished she could use some form of telekinetic power to throw Grace-Marie under a bus. She knew, however, that telekinesis and the supernatural only existed in her favorite shows like *Charmed* and *Buffy*. Buffy was better than Charmed though. *Note to self, must re-watch Buffy soon.*

"Yeah, last night. She gave him the 'she realized her wild parties and boys aren't enough and that she needs something deeper' speech," replied Andrew.

"Well, let's see how long it lasts this time," replied Clara sarcastically. *I could really use a bus right now, bus right now, bus right noooow.*

"I'm not butting in this time," responded Andrew just as Erick and that idiot joined them at the table.

"Hey, guys," said Grace-Marie. "Widad! I really like your shirt, it's so cute!" She continued. "So Erick and I were thinking that maybe we should play *The Game of Life* or something at your place tonight. All of us, I mean. It would be fun to play board games and catch up."

"There's this party, though. I thought we should all go... could be fun," Clara said instantly. She didn't really want to go, but it would beat watching Grace-Marie tongue Erick, using the board game as an excuse

"Yeah. We could play another night... I mean, the semester just started. We can afford to get wasted!" Agreed Andrew.

"Andy, you don't even drink," Erick commented in a rugged yet angelic voice.

"I drink vicariously through Grace-Marie and Clara."

"I think it's a good idea, Clara," Grace-Marie said.

"So, you guys coming to party tonight?" Carmen asked, suddenly appearing from out of nowhere.

"Yes, we are," Clara replied as she quickly realized that instead of watching Grace-Marie molest Erick, she'll spend the night watching Carmen's mating rituals that encompass the entire guest list. *I have no idea why that girl goes to church every Sunday.*

"By the way, Widad, sweetie, you shouldn't eat that much. I'm worried your clothes will suddenly rip apart because they won't be able to contain all of you," commented Carmen viciously as she moseyed away.

"Hey! Carmen, come back and apologize," yelled Clara. She was picturing Grace-Marie's head on Carmen's shoulders at that moment, wishing she could unleash her wrath upon both of them. She never hated anyone as much as she hated both Carmen and Gracie.

Carmen stood still and turned around just as Clara walked the half a meter distance that separated the two of them and grabbed her by the shoulder.

"What did I do?" Carmen asked with innocent puppy eyes that did not fool Clara. But Clara also knew that this was simply the way Carmen acted; it was how her personality was constructed. Carmen was not evil, or so she believed, she simply had a strong defense mechanism that made her seem like she was.

"You honestly didn't notice how much you must have hurt her feelings just now?" Clara asked.

"I didn't hurt her. I just gave her some friendly advice... I mean, she's no Adele!" Carmen commented. "Relax, will you?"

"It's okay, Clara; really, I'm okay. It's Carmen, we're used to her," Widad spoke as she made her way towards Clara and tried to get her back into her seat.

"See? She's okay with it. Anyway, don't forget about tonight." Carmen headed towards the stairs.

Widad was fat; that was true. Truth be told, her features weren't so friendly on the eyes. Still, her esteem needed to be safeguarded because she was quite fragile, and the likes of Carmen would have left her broken so many times if not for Clara.

"She's just a bully, that's all," Andrew said as the two girls returned to their seats. "Wido, I'm sorry about what happened, but you do know we think you look pretty."

"And I can still lose a few calories tonight at the party," Widad commented with a goofy smile.

The Jade Necklace

"Widad, sweetie, you're pretty the way you are... I know it's cliché to say this but there are so many guys who are into fully packaged girls," Grace-Marie intruded. "Who knows? You might meet one of them at the party tonight."

"Which is why, before the party tonight, I'm heading over to your place. When I'm done with you, you're going to be so pretty that there won't be a single boy left who won't drool over you." Clara added in an attempt to hijack the spotlight from Grace-Marie. She had planned to make that offer to Widad anyway, just not in front of everyone else.

Widad was satisfied. "Why not? Let's give it a try."

"I could help out, too, if you girls want," Grace-Marie proposed.

Clara noticed Gracie's hand caress Erick's thigh and lightly stroke his hard on with her index. Erick tried to stop her but she resisted.

"No, it's fine. I can handle this alone," Clara said as she noted the disappointment on Erick's face. *Maybe if you stop thinking with your penile brain, you'd see what a bitch she is.*

"I mean if you really want to join us, I don't mind. But I don't want us to end up crowding her. You know what they say: too many cooks can ruin the meal," she explained.

"I don't mind if you both…" commented Widad.

"It's okay. I guess you girls need some time to bond anyway," Gracie replied nicely. Clara believed that Grace-Marie was just being nice to impress Erick. She was never nice to his gang, and she barely knew they existed up until she dated him. Her own group of friends was known as "the three bitches", and for a good reason: Carmen was one of the three. *Speaking of the three bitches, shouldn't Gracie have been the first to know about the party? Was she playing the "I've changed" card to impress Erick? And if so good job, very convincing!*

"Well, I have to get to class or Montgomery is going to kill me," Andrew said as Clara rolled her eyes because he had never been to her class on time and Montgomery simply happens to be the most sadistic teacher there ever was.

"Andy, it's already too late. I don't think she'll let you in," she said

"I hope not," Andrew said and stood up to walk away.

Andrew was different from Erick even though they had been best friends since school. Erick was a god and Andrew was a closeted feminine twink. Eric was love's slave and Andrew had yet to fall in love. Eric was the object of Clara's desire while Andrew was someone she knew she could check out boys with some day. She knew he was heading into big trouble once he'd reach Montgomery's class but there was nothing she could do. Right now, she had to focus on helping Widad look gorgeous in the evening. She couldn't help but think that she wasn't always this open minded or tolerant of others. However, that changed some time ago when she learned to accept that God, who has created all, must love all of his children.

****

In the evening, Clara knocked on Widad's apartment's door. Widad was lucky enough not to be staying in a university dorm. She had her own room, a bathroom all to herself, and a nice kitchen. The only downside would have been the roommate, but she was also lucky on that front. Fatima was one of the best roommates anyone could ever hope for. Widad opened the door in her cute Anna and Elsa PJs and smiled. *They should have used them more often on Once Upon A Time, they were fun.*

"Hey, sorry I'm a little late... we have to hurry because Erick is picking us up at ten. Where's Fatima?"

The house was quite small and barely had any furniture in it. The corridor that lead up to the quaint living room was not furnished, and the living room only contained two old couches and a small wooden dinner table with four wooden chairs. Facing the couches was a small television set and a DVD player.

"Fatima is studying in her room. I wouldn't advise you to even try saying hello because she'll literally bite your head off." Widad explained as Clara couldn't help but wonder what that girl could possibly have to study during the first week. *Was she memorizing the syllabus?*

"Scary. Let's go to your room then, hurry."

"It's still 8:30 hun. What's the rush?"

"Pretty doesn't materialize in a few seconds Widad. It takes hard work!"

After she finished putting the makeup on Widad's face, she looked at her work of art with pride... Unfortunately, the creation did not share its creator's excitement. Widad looked at her portrait in the mirror with despair written on her forehead.

"I look... nice. Thank you," she said in a dying voice.

Clara looked around the room checking for objects Widad could throw at her She could sense that the girl was more than unhappy with her efforts.

The room was tiny and the white wallpaper was starting to peel off especially around the ceiling but it was still nicer than the rest of the house. There was a small bed with white covers, a small commode with a mirror in front of which they were sitting, and a tiny wooden closet that could barely fit a fifth of Carmen's clothes, Clara imagined.

"You look fabulous," Clara reassured her. "Don't let anyone tell you otherwise." *Widad does look pretty this way, right?*

"But I'm not sure I want to go; I suddenly feel very tired. I think I'm coming down with something."

"Hun, it's just cold feet"

"I'm really not feeling well."

"Widad! Come on! Please! You look pretty! I've worked really hard." The make-up and the shoulder length soft hair truly made Widad look a tad thinner. *Perhaps, she's just shy. She's never looked this pretty before.*

"All right, all right, I'll go."

Clara's cell-phone began ringing with her "Je t'aime" ringtone blasting.

"I thought you hated romantic music. Especially French, Lara Fabian kind of romantic music."

"Well, I do... but Erick loves it and this is his ringtone." She hung up on him because she assumed he was waiting downstairs. "Come on, he's waiting for us."

"I'll be out in a minute. I need to use the bathroom. I think it'll take a while," Widad said as she rushed out of the room.

"Widad, you're going to the party even if I have to drag you there!"

"Yes, okay. Just go to the car. I'll be out in a minute," Widad said as Clara realized that her friend might have Irritable Bowel Syndrome on top of all her troubles. She didn't understand why a sane person would instantly think of medical difficulties right before a party but couldn't help herself. IBS meant that a person might suffer from diarrhea or constipation or both in stressful situation. *Poor Wido!* Perhaps it was better not to let Widad onto these thoughts, just in case she does have it. She wouldn't be able to handle the stress.

****

The four friends and the evil bitch from hell, Grace-Marie, found themselves at the party, which took place at Shereen's villa just outside of Beirut. The house was splendid from the outside: all white with water fountains and green gardens filled with roses and bushes. Clara had never been there before and she couldn't help but wish that she had lived in a house like that. As they reached the front door, they found that it was open. The inside of the villa was even better than the outside. There were at least three interconnected living rooms filled with dancing young adults, booze and loud music, and stairs that led upstairs to where the orgies (that Shereen was famous for) took place. The moment they stepped inside they couldn't help but stare at Carmen, already flaunting her naturally absurd behavior.

She danced erotically with three men... at the same time. In fact, she was seductively making eye contact with every man around. As she danced, Carmen climbed on the table and drank a beer very erotically, spilling some of it on her barely covered breasts. Then she slammed the bottle to the ground and it shattered to pieces. The three men lifted her up in the air. Rising above all the other guests, she grabbed a beer from a random passerby. The men placed her on the black bar that separated one of the numerous kitchens from the living room. One of the three leaned back, placing his head between her spiked heels, just as she bent towards him and poured the drink into his mouth, half smiling and winking at the gang.

"Guys, I need to use the bathroom. Be right back." Widad ran.

"Want me to come with you?" Clara asked.

"Well I..." muttered Widad when Carmen arrived and cut in.

"What is that smell? God! Widad what did you eat honey?"

"I...I..."

"Sweetie, for your own good, what are you doing to yourself?"

"Carmen, will you cut it out? Stop talking to her and go away, now!" Clara confronted her fake nemesis, leaving the true one to plant soft kisses on Erick's neck.

"I'm just stating the obvious. It's not like you all haven't thought it!" argued Carmen ignoring everything Clara said.

"I have to go," said Widad as she rushed upstairs.

Widad gone, Carmen proposed to play truth or dare. Clara wanted nothing to do with her but saint Grace-Marie wanted to play, which is how they found themselves seated in a circle upstairs in a Louis the 14th style bedroom amongst people they were not exactly fans of. On the bright side, Widad had come back and their pack was whole. Carmen spun the bottle and appointed herself as host of the game.

"Looks like it's our little Andy versus big Wido." Carmen giggled.

"Truth," said Andrew.

"What is it you hate most about me?" Widad asked as she lowered her eyes.

"That's… I… Nothing. There's nothing, I… well, actually there is something. You are a great person, Widad, but you let people run over you. And that's what I dislike most about you. I dislike the fact that you don't allow yourself to get what you deserve in life."

"Wow, how touching." Carmen whispered thoughtfully. "Next!" she suddenly squealed as she spun the bottle another time.

The Jade Necklace

"Well, Grace-Marie, what would you like from Erick? Truth or dare?" asked Carmen.

"Truth, I want him to ask me if I think he's cute," Grace-Marie said as Erick gave her a most predictable smile.

"Do you think I'm cute?" asked Erick.

"No," she replied as he looked her sarcastically in the eye. "I think you're hot."

A few spins later, it was Erick's turn to be dared by his girlfriend.

"I want dare, but I hope you dare me to kiss you, sexy," said Erick.

"I dare you to.... Kiss me."

As their lips interlocked, Clara chose to stare away.

Carmen spun the bottle again and this time it was Carmen's turn to be dared by Grace Marie.

"Truth," Carmen said.

"Pick one person in this room you would have sex with," Gracie asked.

"You have a very dirty mind. Let me see, hmmm... I think I would do chubby dark and ugly sitting next to you. What's your name again?" she asked.

"Marc, bitch... Every man knows that any dick is good enough for your pussy, whore," he said.

"I could tell from the lump in your jeans when we were dancing that you wouldn't mind doing me. But, as you said any dick would do, too bad the lump was only your giant clit," she said as the boy got up and left, which made Andrew smile.

Marc had always attempted to bully Andrew and, for him to be bullied instead for a change brought a little joy to Clara's heart. The boy was chubby. His hair was black and short. His ears and nose were too large and disproportional with the rest of his features and his eyes were embellished with huge bags.

"Ok, looks like it's me and you Grace-Marie... again... truth or dare?" Carmen asked after she spun again.

"Dare."

"I dare you to... kiss me passionately... on the lips," Carmen said, shocking most of them.

Erick smiled. Clara was certain that he thought his girlfriend wasn't going to do it. He gave her too much credit. He probably smiled because he was flattered.

"Carmen, is there something you would like to tell us?" Erick asked attempting to thwart the awkwardness of the dare.

"In case anyone is wondering, I'm not a lesbian but I feel like being experimental tonight."

"You're not going to kiss her are you?" Widad asked as she saw Grace-Marie lean in on Carmen.

"Why not?" Grace-Marie said as she smoothly placed her lips upon Carmen's. She delicately caressed them with hers before they were devoured by Carmen whose hands were clutched around Grace-Marie's head. Neither would let go of the embrace. Carmen slowly leaned backwards as Grace-Marie followed in a synchronized motion. She laid over her gently, caressing her hair, kissing her soft juicy lips. Gracie eventually let go to seek oxygen, only to be shocked to see the stupor on everybody's face and, most importantly, the erection in every boy's jeans. The girls giggled as they took their places in the circle while everyone continued staring at them with riddled eyes. It was in that moment that Erick stood up enraged and walked away. He headed outside as Clara quickly followed. Gracie didn't even budge. She just continued to laugh playfully. Clara couldn't reach her prince in time. She saw him driving away from the villa.

Clara stood on the sidewalk and was trying to reach his cell-phone when she saw a black man walk towards her.

He was large, tall, muscular and as black as the night that engulfed them. She couldn't easily discern his features in the dark but assumed that he must have been some exchange student, a classmate. There was no cause for alarm.

"Do you have a ciggie?" He asked in a deep voice.

"No, nonsmoker," she replied before she dialed Erick's number again.

"Are you okay? Did something happen to you?" He asked politely as he tried to put his hand on her shoulder.

"No. thanks for asking," she answered rudely, quickly moving his hand away.

"Hello, Erick, could you please come back? We can talk about what happened and... you're kind of our ride home."

When Erick answered with approval she hung up and started back towards the villa.

"I'm Lex and you are?" The stranger asked, following her.

"Not interested," she snapped, noticing that he was still there.

She quickened her pace, somewhat afraid of her new acquaintance. The main iron-gate was open but there was no one outside.

"That's rude. Didn't your mother teach you to show some respect to strangers?" Lex asked.

But she kept on walking until he grabbed her arm. She instantly turned back and kicked him in the balls, then fled. Her heart raced; she heard the crunching of gravel beneath his boots and did not dare look back. She tried to head back to the party but he quickly blocked her path, so she found herself forced to run the other way.

She quickly noticed Erick's car pass by as she turned a corner and wished that he would have seen her.

Clara ran for the backdoor but found a dead end instead. The backdoor was locked and shut, the kitchen lights were off and a wall blocked her path forward. She had no choice but to go back but Lex was blocking her exit.

In a shaking voice she said: "what do you want?

"How considerate of you to ask." He laughed. She tried to break down the door but to no avail as she wasn't strong enough.

"Is this some sick joke?" She said backing away from the door.

"Life is a joke! What I want is... you."

He approached her slowly. She tried to flee but he grabbed her by the hair. He shoved her against a wall, choking her with one hand and feeling her with the other. Clara had almost given up when Erick called her name.

"Clara!" He cried out. "Hey! Who the fuck are you? Pick on someone your own size, you fucking bastard!"

"More fun." Lex said, pushing Clara to the ground. He kicked her once in the stomach. Tasting blood and asphalt, she looked up. *My hero!*

Erick charged at him with all his strength but Lex dodged him and Erick crashed into the wall.

"You're fun," he said when he rushed towards him like a bullet, and kicked him in the stomach. He then grabbed the boy by his hair and suddenly pulled out a cold blade placing it upon Eric's throat. Clara's blood began to boil and she began to remember the house on fire, the pain in her shoulders, and the devil that saved her.

She could not let Erick die; she loved him. Erick had suffered enough for one night. She would not let him be killed like that, in some alley by some pervert called Lex who seemed to be capable of cold blooded murder.

It was then she felt a jolt of energy leave her body and Lex was thrown into the wall. When Erick managed to get to his feet, he saw that there was no one there, no way to explain what had happened. She didn't understand it either. *Did I do that?*

"Looks like the little girl is packing some juice," Lex said as his gaze moved to her. She trembled yet still fixed her eyes on him. If she had done what she thought she had just done then she was the only way for them to get out of this mess. She had to focus all of her energy on Lex in order to do it again so they could flee. As he paced towards her she tried to move him with her mind again but found that she couldn't. Looking at his face, she noticed the strangest thing about his eyes. *Yellow with oval pupils: like a cat's.* Lex was almost upon her and she froze remembering the man in black and the attackers. However, Erick had managed to get back up and shoved Lex out of the way into the dumpster. Clara instantly sprung to her feet and ran towards Erick.

Hand in hand, with Clara trailing behind her prince, they made their way to his car as Lex chased them. The moment they got in, Erick drove right into the man who had rushed towards them at full speed. The car didn't touch him. Lex leaped unnaturally. By the time they reached the end of the street, he was nowhere to be seen. *Was he on top of the car?*

Erick sped up and hit the brakes suddenly just in case the man was clinging to the car. But Lex was nowhere. He was gone. *Did he work for the man in black?*

"I'm calling the cops," said Erick.

"No!"

"Why? You know him?" he said.

"Of course not... but..."

"How did he get off me? Did you do that?" he asked.

"I don't know."

"He said that it was you. Is that why you don't want me to talk to the police? Clara, what' going on?"

Chapter Four: Gargoyle

A flood of distorted sounds and images – echoes of swords clanging, severed heads covered in ash after battle, mothers eating their children, snakes slithering out of a rotten vagina.

It took him a while to find himself.

"Bader..."

"Yes."

"Take me."

He woke up in a small cell, a cage that he barely fit in. He had to keep his head bent when standing up.

His cage hung from the ceiling in the middle of a room that, with its humid walls, appeared to be underground.

The bars of the cage glowed of a strange red *(like blood on fire, like burning lips)*, and he was reluctant to touch them.

The room was empty except for a couple of wooden chairs. Georges, the bald man who had captured him the previous day, sat on one of them with a coffee mug in one hand. Seeing Bader rise from his slumber, the bald man did not move nor speak. There was power in his silence. And, for a moment, Bader felt like a canary bird. *Waiting for me to chirp and tweet for you, asshole?*

"What do you want?" He growled at the bald man. *When free, eat bird owners.*

"Don't worry, my friend. We don't plan on hurting you." George assured him.

But Bader knew that was a lie. He was their captive, whoever they were, and cages were not usually reserved for honorable guests.

"Who sent you?" Bader spoke assertively. He could not show fear nor weakness. Not that he was afraid, of course.

"You know, gargoyles are fascinating creatures... uhm... statues by day, flesh eating creatures by night. But you, you are a man by day, and that is very interesting." Georges spoke while he circled the cage.

"Gargoyles?" He laughed, attempting to sound ignorant but knew that the soon-to-be-dead bald man was well aware of what he was.

"Darla, the girl that you savagely brutalized, had a vision. She saw what you truly are. So, Bader, my good fellow, I have to ask you: how is it that you can now pass as a human?"

"And I must ask, too. How come Darla has so much power? Seers tend to be weak." He spoke seriously. "Her mouth is like a Hoover! She's not a seer, is she? She's something far more special, a swallower." *That ought to show strength.*

Bader's had a gut feeling about Darla. She was certainly special, exceptional even. But he could not place his finger on what she was.

"Let me remind you that *you* are the guest here. You will answer my questions and..." Georges was getting angry, and angry people make mistakes. But his anger, Bader was amazed, was also balanced.

"And then you'd let the monster that's been terrorizing this city walk free?"

"Perhaps fasting will lighten your soul, my friend," Georges smiled.

"Perhaps bashing your head into a wall would make you a better gentleman," Bader answered back.

"Listen, I want to know how many gargoyles are still out there and how many have this ability of yours," Georges resumed.

"Gargoyles are extinct."

"If you've been hiding out in plain sight, then so have others... I want answers." He sipped from his mug.

"Ask Darla to find your answers in her visions then ... *Dick*... If you're right about me being a gargoyle, then I'm sure you must know that gargoyles have incredible strength and speed. They can bend iron, break stone walls, and they can rip your heart out before you can say please. I might have gone easy on the bitch, but I'm going to show you what a gargoyle can really do." He grabbed two of the bars to pry them apart.

The pain hit him like none he had ever felt before. He fell. His extremities were numb with pain and breathing became a labored chore. He attempted to stand up, fell, and did not try again for some time.

It was another minute before he regained mobility but by then the bald douche bag had left. The bars must have been equipped with some strange technology that was meant to tame him.

He would not dare touch the bars again. There was no escape. And as the hours turned into days, his hunger became unquenchable. By night, he couldn't sleep away his metamorphosis. Once changed, he couldn't help but feel the agony of a thousand volts surge through his body as his larger monstrous form could not fit in the small containment that was the cage. The pain would turn him back into a man momentarily and then the vicious cycle would keep on repeating itself all night long.

Long ago, before he could master his nature, he was forced to turn into a beast every night. He had access to unimaginable strength in his beastly form that he could not attain in his human skin. True, as a human he was powerful, fast and agile but as a monster he had the strength of a hundred men if not more. It was thanks to Agnes - the scullery maid who raised him - that he managed to douse the beast within. She had taught him that whenever he remained calm or went to sleep the creature could be locked away in the depth of his being. However, in this cage the monster was unleashed, but, even with his excess strength, he could not break through the bars. He knew that if his bestial form could not even overcome this cell, then there was nothing he could do. All hope was lost and then one morning, Darla came.

"Hello Darla, what brings you here?" He spoke sarcastically as if welcoming her to his humble abode.

He didn't bother standing up but merely shifted to his side. Thankfully, there was enough space for him to lie down which had allowed him to get a few minutes of sleep from time to time, as long as he wouldn't roll and come in contact with the bars.

Darla wore a "come fuck-me" black skirt and a short tank top that didn't entirely cover her massive tits. Did she come to tease him one last time? If she did, it was working, he was hard. He hadn't had a woman in days and wanted to let off steam at all cost. He wanted to break free, pin her face against the wall, strip her and ride her tight asshole for hours.

"I should've killed you," he said calmly.

"What stopped you? I saw you eat that man in my vision. Why didn't you kill me? Why did you let me go?" She approached his cell and spoke gently.

"Because all my life I have been searching for someone like you. You are my soul mate. I love you, Carla, or was it Darla?" He then cracked up laughing.

"I've had too much pussy and ass in my life to remember all of the names and that's what you are baby… one hot piece of ass that I fucked."

He laughed. She grinned. He couldn't tell what she was thinking. Was she going to use their strange technology to inflict pain on him again? He did not know nor care. He was dead; they weren't going to let him go, he knew that now. But, negative thinking was for the weak and he had gotten out of worse situations in his time.

"Why am I still alive?" She asked sincerely trying to maintain eye contact.

"Feeling guilty are we? I save you and you send your soon-to-be-dead friend after me!" He mocked her.

"You are a natural born killer. I've seen what you can do," she argued.

"I should've snapped your neck right then and there," his gaze pierced her eyes and he knew that she could sense the seriousness of his claim.

"I believe you're not like the other gargoyles. Whatever you've done to gain a human form must be affecting you. You must be tapping into human emotion. I believe you can be saved." She approached his cage and looked up at him as she spoke.

"So you want to help me?" He did not move and fixed his eyes upon her.

"Yes..."

"In all my years, and I've had many, this is the first time that someone actually believes in me. Thank you. I am really grateful," he lied.

"You didn't let me die. There's goodness in you."

"Help me find it, will you?" He gazed into her eyes and thought that the time had come to put an end to the current farce.

"I will. I promise," she said with a coy half smile. A lock of auburn hair fell to her face and with her index finger, she tucked it behind her ear.

He began to laugh hysterically. Her freckles masked the red of her anger as he noticed them for the first time.

"You stupid cunt." He continued to laugh. "How gullible do you think I am? If it weren't for these bars I'd show you just how much goodness there is in me. Or do you want me to believe that you think this is some kind of fairytale? The beauty who tamed the beast? "

"Bastard... if you won't cooperate, they are going to torture you. It'll never end. You're immortal. You're in for decades of suffering .We just want to know how your species pulled this off. We thought you were..." Her hands were shaking.

"Extinct... Well, if I answer your questions, what's to stop you from making me extinct? Who are you people anyway?"

"I'll tell you if you cooperate." She tried to affirm her presence but he knew better. She was still a scared little girl trying to satisfy the bald man.

"I am very intrigued ... Deal...Nah, I'll pass... don't give a fuck about you all...Leave." His voice was coarse for he truly had had enough.

"I promise I won't let them hurt you." Her pupils had dilated again and the right side of his lip pulled into a half smile all on its own.

"I promise I will tear you to pieces with my claws." *Perhaps not scary enough considering what went down the last time I tried.*

The power went out, the bars no longer glowed and the alarm sounded at a distance. They were in the dark but he could see as if it were midday. He was underground but could sense that night had fallen and he could turn into the flying blight of London again. Once again, she was an easy prey. He pried the bars apart and stepped out of the cage, landing on the ground with a thud.

The innocent were never his to kill, even though he was hungry. She backed away from him as her eyes slowly adjusted. But she was soon startled by the rattling they could hear coming from upstairs.

"What's happening?" he inquired calmly.

"We're under attack." she said, her heart racing.

"Who's attacking you freaks?"

"Someone more dangerous than you."

The Jade Necklace

Chapter Five: The Savior

This is the work that I'm supposed to do; such is the will of God. I didn't choose my calling – it was presented to me six years ago – and I most certainly could not reject it.

Chaos is our world's one and only queen. She is a cancer growing in the hearts of men. God and religion both agree on that. The world is heading into entropy, science says.

"The great day of the Lord is near, near and hastening fast; the sound of the day of the Lord is bitter; the mighty man cries aloud there. A day of wrath is that day, a day of distress and anguish, a day of ruin and devastation,

a day of darkness and gloom, a day of clouds and thick darkness."

The Lord is my shepherd. My faith guides me. Other men are misguided. They lead petty lives where all they care for are the pleasures of the flesh. Most people live out their lives on this earth with no real purpose. They are void. They seek nothing but mundane pleasures. They awaken into the world, grow older and die like insects. But what lies in between?

Young man grows up, goes to work, marries a woman, has children, and dies.

Young man grows up, fights for his country, and dies on the battlefield.

Young woman grows up, cannot make ends meet, turns to prostitution, and dies of tertiary syphilis.

All their stories are the same. They all fit into one of the dozen possible scenarios. Not one person's journey is unique. Yet they live on, completely oblivious to their purpose on earth. No one cares for the Lord anymore. No one is concerned with justice, except those who are oppressed and treated unjustly – even *they* are unwilling to act. No one cares about love anymore – that true, selfless love towards our fellow men. We have become ghouls, yet the Lord hasn't given up on us. His day will come. But first, a few souls need to be sacrificed for the greater good.

From the perspective of men, I am a cold-hearted killer, a monster. But from God's perspective, I am a hero, a martyr sacrificing his eternal soul for the greater good. A killer must go to hell, after all, even if he does God's work. But that is a sacrifice I would gladly make for the greater good.

I can still remember the faces of those I have killed in His name, they haunt me. Those victims might see me as a villain. But they don't know of my suffering, the suffering that their pains have brought upon me.

I dream at night of the look on that Frenchman's face when I wrecked his life in minutes. He must think me soulless. He certainly hates me.

His girlfriend Arije was barely over twenty, studying medicine in France. One night, she sat in front of her chimney carefully studying the fire and was caught in a trance. I had been watching her with my mind's eye before the attack. She could have been thinking of her life ahead, of the love she felt towards her Francois, of the loved ones she left behind to move to Paris. That is something I'll never know. One thing I knew for certain was that she was filthy rich, otherwise she wouldn't have been able to afford such a large apartment in Paris all by herself.

I paced slowly towards her door then knocked gently. She rushed to answer it. She must have thought that it was her lover outside. She was surprised when she found me instead, a tall man in a black cloak.

I grabbed her by the neck and elevated her body, her feet no longer set on the ground. I do not possess any super human strength, I was merely channeling her own. She closed her eyes and teleported into the kitchen where I rematerialized, still chocking her. She must have assumed I just happened to have the same powers that she had but, in fact, I was *wind* and I could mimic all of her abilities when near her.

Three pincers dug deep into my skin. Blood. The bitch had scratched me. I was forced to let go. She fell on her two feet and punched me in the groin. The pain was unbearable and made me wish I were born a woman. I had made that wish in vain throughout my childhood but, alas, I am a man.

Then, I heard her lover. He must have found the front door open.

"Arije? Où es tu?" he asked probably making his way towards the kitchen.

"Francois!" she yelled as she disappeared into thin air.

"What ze....! Comment, t'as fais ça?" She had appeared before him in the living room. The stupid girl could have fled anywhere but she wanted to save him. I gathered my strength and made my way towards them both.

I never wanted to kill her in his presence. But there was no turning back. Still, I spared him after taking her life in front of his eyes; although, now I think that it would've been better if I had killed them both. No man should outlive his loved ones.

I now stand in front of a small flower shop on an empty street. I know for certain what lies beneath the flowery facade. I have shared salt and bread with the very people we're about to assault. I have loved one of them, too. But there's work to be done, and there's always a chance that one or two of us might die. There's thunder, then the sky begins to pour. My companions are with me, and they are ready to express the Lord's will on this earth, as am I.

Rain: it washes everything, cleanses everything, but its effects are limited. Rain cannot change the world, it cannot wash away intolerance, it cannot give the throne of hate to love, and it cannot forge change in the laws of society and nature. But, as I am the Lord's instrument, I can.

"Jonathan, what are we waiting for?" The dark haired beauty standing beside me asks. Her eyes had an unspeakable darkness that reflected that of her soul; however, she is a necessary evil. Like me, she will be punished for her deeds when the Lord's Day comes. She wears the revealing red dress of a lethal siren though she is nothing more than a witch. Her name is Isabelle and she is, to me, the whore of Babylon; a necessary evil that reveals itself when the "end of days" comes.

We are seven companions standing in front of "Mikey's Flower Shop". But in spite of our limited number that symbolizes the number of days it took the lord to create the earth, we are a force to be reckoned with. Isabelle is a beautiful witch and my most lethal weapon. She is earth.

Ahmad is an Iraqi man who worships the Lord my way. He stands by my side for he is a most capable warrior of the Lord. I converted him not long ago and baptized him in the Euphrates. He believes in our most noble cause. As he stands beside me, his height barely reaching up to my elbow, I realize how valuable he could be. Skinny and short, they will underestimate what he can do. But Ahmad is *fire* and fire consumes all.

Cyril, a tall and muscular Frenchman, stands beside me on the other side. I do not trust those hooded green eyes of his for he is too reckless. All blonds are non-conformists, I have learned throughout my life. Every man with a goatee is a trouble maker, I had come to realize. The proof came in the form of Cyril who has both. He fits the stereotype perfectly by often disobeying my orders. But, at least he tries to do what's right and that alone makes him part of our little family. He is wind like me.

By Cyril, drenched in water, stands Jin. He is water and one of his greatest defensive abilities is shape-shifting... He can even change into a dragon if needed! The scaly dragon makes up for his short stature and lack of facial hair. He grew up in a small fishing village off the coast of Japan until he came to realize the full scope of his powers. It was then that the Lord sent me his way and I taught him everything he knows. He's been like a little brother ever since.

Behind us stand Isabelle and Jared. He is earth but in no way as powerful as Isabelle. I sometimes wonder why we let him join us in such missions. He is too much of a hog to be able to move around. We let him join us mainly because of his small wand that makes him a level 2 witch capable of casting various sorts of spells. Some of his spells go wrong: the latest being his previously hazel eyes taking on a yellow tint that happened to go well with his black hair which had been mistakenly set on fire a few months ago.

Last but not least, there's Vladimir, a vampire. He stands tall next to Ahmad, his face a blank canvas. He knows that he is an abomination that walks the earth and wishes to make penance for his greatest sin of all:

existing. His almond-black eyes are fixed on the flower shop, probably thinking of the task at hand. He is the most handsome among our party for his body was sculpted in a way that would make Michelangelo's David die of spite but I must not dwell on that. Vladimir was different than other creatures of the night. He could walk in the sunlight thanks to Isabelle's magic: she forged him a daylight necklace that he wears at all times. It is made of gold with a V-shaped pendant. Vladimir was not the run of a mill vampire - he was a pure blood and that made him stronger than most of his kind. This allowed him to assume a different winged form whenever he willed it but he seldom resorted to it seeing that it took a toll on the "humanity" left within him. To change form would mean for him to succumb to the urges of the animal within, to let the animal take over and to allow himself to become its instrument. He never changed before us nor since he met us for he knew that he risked never being able to regain control. Once a man tastes the darkness it is hard to let it go.

We are seven companions on a mission to do our Lord's work. Our Lord is just, loving, and forgiving and cares for nothing but the wellbeing of His children that strive on the earth, even if these very children are destroying his kingdom out of greed and ignorance. That is why He sent us, to save them, to do what needs to be done.

We are all still standing in front of "Mickey's Flower Shop". The streets are as silent and empty as they could be. The lights in the flower shop are off. We cannot see what's inside, but we know what awaits us: battle and carnage.

I give the order and we march towards it. Ahmad opens the door with a wave of his hand and we all march in. An alarm sounds. The store is dark but seems to be made of a small maze of flowers with a counter opposite the entrance and a door that leads to a *supposed storage unit* right below. But I know what truly lies behind that door: the headquarters of the Brotherhood of the Dawn. They are a group of men and women who sought out and protected mages and have now become the guardians of many phoenixes. They have four phoenixes in this very place that are being trained and protected as we speak. I must destroy them along with those protecting them. This is what God wants. All Phoenixes must die, starting with the ones that are members of the brotherhood: Darla, Jacob, Meriam and

Juan. The difference between these and the rest is that they've had months of training. They have learned to access powers mere mages wouldn't even dream of. To defeat the phoenixes under the protection of the brotherhood would make the hunt for the rest seem trivial in comparison.

A large man comes out from the secret entrance and, with a swift hand gesture, Ahmad snaps his neck telekinetically.

God has willed this death. I must not kill the innocent but must kill all those who stand in His glorious path. Phoenixes must all perish.

"And it came to pass that night that the angel of the Lord went out, and smote in the camp of the Assyrians a hundred fourscore and five thousand: and when they arose early in the morning, behold, they were all dead corpses."

Their security cameras must have detected us so we must move quickly. I signal my men to break and we walk through the door one by one. I go first and come upon darkness. But I know what lies in this darkness for I have lived here before. These stairs lead to the sanctuary, a sanctuary that the family I was once a part of created. Isabelle stands tall behind me and utters her magical words. Her wand illuminates the way and we go down the steep stairs.

Her wand is the source of her power for she is a level 2 witch who can only practice wand magic. Her golden wand is shaped like two intertwining snakes; one with red ruby eyes and the other with green eyes. On top of the head of each snake rests a small crown made of jade. Jared's wand, on the other hand, is made of Cedar wood and merely looks like a stick. Even though he is a level 2 witch as well, he isn't nearly as powerful. Part of her strength comes from her wand for it is ancient and few witches ever possessed such wands.

As we go down the stairs, two men attack with firearms. But before they can act, fire gushes out of Ahmad's fingers and incinerates them. I feel truly sorry for them, both sorry and guilty. But there's no time for such feelings for they interfere with the mission.

We reach the end of the stairs where another door stands before us. Ahmad opens it. As a bearer of the Fire element, Ahmad had been lucky enough to have three active abilities. He was capable of telekinesis, pyrokenesis and incredible strength; skills that I always used as my own when in his vicinity. I had no special powers of my own, foresight, astral projection and dream walking aside. But I could tap into anyone else's powers and use them as I will.

We move in. I explain to my companions that not more than fifty people inhabit this place and that we must separate to get to the phoenixes. I give them direct orders not to harm any who do not strike first. Ahmad stands guard at the gate that leads to the main stairway and is instructed to let anyone, who isn't a phoenix and docile, pass. The rest of us split into two groups that are to head in opposite directions along the long corridor. I attempt to see the phoenixes' whereabouts with my mind's eye but cannot. They seem to be shielded by a powerful spell down here. Cyril, Jared and I head north. The insides of the building are just as I remember them: beautiful white walls and limestone tiles to match with narrow corridors that could not fit more than three men at a time. The long corridor runs in a circle and many doors decorate its wall. The doors lead to the different bedrooms of the tenants and we have to search them one by one for phoenixes. Both ends of the long corridors lead to a great hall where the members of this family would gather for special occasions or common dinners. The great hall had a kitchen under it as well as a large library, a meeting room, a cell, and a security room. All of these could be accessed without having to go to the grand hall via the many doors found around us.

We search the first few rooms and find them to be empty. Of course, they know we are here. I know they're all in the great hall and if we're to win, the seven of us will have to defeat fifty of our equals. The odds seem to be at their side but for one thing, Cyril and I are capable of accessing any ability that any one of them has which tips the scale to our side. Our element is all too rare and no one here possesses it.

We approach the great hall and I see him, my lover, standing before us with the same confidence and strength I've always known him to have. It's been five years since the last time I've seen him but he still looks the same. He is bald now but still has the same green eyes, like doors to his soul. He has always been a proud, strong man, a guardian of all that he holds dear. I cannot dare look him in the eyes for I am about to take away everything he has set out to protect. Everything we had once sworn to protect is about to fall apart because of my own doing and here I am standing before him unable to utter a single word. I have won or will win but know in my heart the bitter taste that this victory will bring.

"You have to go through me."

Georges knows all too well that I cannot kill him, will not kill him. I truly wish him no harm for he and I have always had a special bond but this must be done. He was my one true love before I found God, my personal savior.

"Leave this place Johnny."

He still thinks of me as Johnny. I have to get rid of him; he reminds me too much of the person I used to be. Yet, I find myself walking towards him.

"I'm sorry, Georges."

I walk slowly, unable to meet his gaze, and I gently touch his hand. I remember the first time I ever saw him. We were ten, going to the same school in San Francisco and I hated his guts. He used to tease me in front of everyone. He went as far as making me cry once, even beat me. It was the seventies and it was expected of him to hate faggots. It was long before Harvey Milk fought valiantly for equal rights and in spite of his butch exterior, as butch as it could get for a ten year old, he was a docile coward. It was easy for him to hate me then and he loved the way it made him feel normal, the way it helped him fit in the crowd. It wasn't until years later that he realized that what he was truly hating was the "him" that he saw in me.

I now know, however, the reason why the Lord created homosexuality. It is a test, just like the forbidden fruit. He created this need in me to want other men but did not fail to inform me that it was a sin to act upon these desires. He wanted to test my faith, to see if I was strong enough to resist such a temptation, strong enough to earn the kingdom of heaven. I used to be weak and lost but with the Lord, his help, I have found my way again. My faith will not waver again.

"Johnny, this is not the will of God. God is love and tolerance, God is forgiveness..."

Jared, cast a spell to send him away from here; somewhere far away. But keep him safe.

Jared answers my telepathic request with haste and as his wand glows with a bright light at its edge, the one I love only second to God fades away in mid speech. This way he can be safe from what I've become.

Now to the inevitable massacre of all those who will oppose us in the grand hall.

I could ask Jared to try and teleport anyone who wasn't a phoenix away from here, but why waste his energy? We should smite down our enemies without mercy! We move in and find more than thirty men and women prepared to fight for their lives.

"Anyone who is not a phoenix is free to go. I'm only here for Jacob, Darla, Juan and Meriam. Give them up and you can all go."

They maintain their offensive position and I know that their deaths are inevitable. That is when Isabelle, Vladimir and Jin arrive from the other side.

"I'm sorry, my friends."

Kill them. I bid my followers.

Chapter Six: Run

Fear was all too apparent in Darla's eyes- it made Bader realize how dangerous their foe was. They were in the basement but were very well aware of the chaos that reigned above. So many noises were heard, noises of people shouting, screaming, and crying, noises of glass shattering, hurried footsteps, and pleas for help! The clash above was culminating into a symphony of war louder than the ones he'd heard during World War 2. She steadily and slowly backed away from him trying to make for the stairs.

"I won't hurt you. If I wanted to, you'd be dead already," he said.

She kept her silence but stopped moving.

"Is there any way out?" He asked.

"I have to help them."

"I don't think you can."

"The only way out is through that door." She rushed up the stairs and he followed. He wasn't going to let the stupid bitch do anything unintelligent and get herself killed. *She's too hot to die.*

They ran out of the cell through a long dark corridor until they reached another set of stairs with dozens of steps. She went up and he followed after her. The moment she opened the door that led out of the basement, they saw the carnage. Inside a large assembly room, twice the size of any he'd seen before, was an ensuing fight that seemed more like a massacre. A young Hispanic girl cried under one of the many rectangular tables that lined the great hall. A large man jumped high into the air to avoid a fireball and clung to the outsized golden chandelier. The fireball crashed into a young girl at the back end of the hall and burnt its way out through her skin. The scene was an array of mutilated corpses, fallen tables and chairs, and bloodied white walls! He immediately covered her mouth so that she wouldn't scream at the sight of her dead friends. She fought him and merely let out a muffled shout as the tears rushed down her face. He pulled her back into the basement's stairs and closed the door hoping that the warring parties did not notice them.

"We need to go," he whispered in her ear and she nodded. He took his hand off her mouth.

"We have to find my sister."

She broke free and rushed out. As he followed, he couldn't help but notice a strange man who stood upside down on the ceiling. Blood dribbled from his long sharp nails, as he landed on the body of the man that had fallen on the ground right under him. *A vampire?* The vampire jumped off the ceiling and landed on the man's torso. His sharp nails swiftly drew lines of red across his victim's neck.

Darla was frozen in time, frantically scanning the room with her eyes. When the vampire noticed them and rushed their way at full speed, she did not budge. Bader morphed into his monstrous self and with one punch sent the vampire flying into the wall.

"Run," he growled, waking her from her trance.

"No!"

She screamed as she attacked an Asian man trying to beat a young girl who wore her fair hair in a ponytail. The girl couldn't have been older than fifteen and she resembled Darla very much. She was cowering on the ground in her catholic school girl uniform. The tears rolled down her cheeks, but as soon as Darla came for her, the girl found the strength to stand up. *That must be her sister.* With one kick to the face, the Asian fell to the ground. The Asian rolled away, ripped his shirt off and morphed into a giant beast. It was double Bader's size, scathed, black as night with blood red eyes. Its razor sharp teeth protruded out of its mouth. Its growl echoed through the entire room as its pointed tail cut into another nearby man's torso. *He must be water.* That man could harness his defensive powers into shifting into a dragon-like beast whenever he wanted. *Cool Power.*

People were fighting everywhere around them but Bader's focus was fixated on Darla's debacle. He ran towards her in order to protect her but was knocked down. The man who knocked him down was Herculean in strength, tall, and well built. He had blond hair, blue eyes, and a goatee of fire. The herculean man telekinetically pinned Bader against the opposite wall and charged towards him. Darla, meanwhile, grabbed her sister's hand and pulled her away from the monster.

However, with one swift movement of his tail, they were both on the ground. It was because of mere chance that they didn't come into contact with the pointed end of his evil tail.

The Herculean man was on Bader now, his left hand punching Bader's face while a fireball formed in his right. Moments before the fire ball touched his skin, Bader managed to free his arm and grab the Herculean man's head, snapping his neck. He was then free from his strong grip. But seconds had not passed before Bader was attacked again by the vampire, who had jumped off the chandelier and moved at missile speed. Bader instantly ducked, dodging the blow. He glanced at Darla who had pushed her sister out of harm's way but was now facing the monster herself.

Bader's wings spread, but before he could flap them and jet past the commotion to reach her, the vampire grabbed him by the legs and tossed him into a wall. The vampire then rushed at him and repeatedly punched him on the ribs. *Vampires aren't supposed to be that strong.*

Bader, trapped between long-nailed fingers, could smell smoke. The place was on fire. A woman, with a glowing wand shaped like two snake heads, was uttering inaudible words that seemed to create a gigantic sphere of fire, water, dirt and air around the entire confinement. The insides of the hall were erupting in flame.

He rolled onto the ground to escape the vampire and hurried towards the woman with the wand. It seemed that stopping her was essential in order to prevent the horrible carnage. But the vampire was on him again, on his back. Bader's face hit the floor and he was pinned to the ground.

"I thought gargoyles were powerful creatures," the vampire mocked. "You're far too easy."

Bader saw that Darla had found her feet and jumped on the Asian monster's back. However, the beast stood on its hind paws and, with a jerking motion, sent her flying across the room into a pile of broken tables and chairs. Darla's sister found her way towards her and shook her awake. The room was getting dimmer; people were suffocating from the thick smoke and falling to the ground one after the other. Darla's comrades were hopeless. The invaders were too powerful.

Two fangs dup deep into Bader's neck and his thick blood trickled down his neck. The vampire was too strong but he had to take him. Meanwhile, on the other side of the room, the Asian monster was still attacking Darla. Her sister was screaming, when the pointed end of his tale hit Darla in the shoulder.

Then something happened. A strange electrical current flew out of Darla's fingers and zapped the Asian monster off of her. She then did the same to the vampire who fell helpless to the ground as well. *Couldn't she have done that from the start?* However, a mage's powers come from her emotions and it is possible that Darla had instantly acquired this new ability, one that she couldn't access before. Otherwise, she would have also used it on him back at his place, when they first met.

She and her sister crawled to Bader's side, blood gushing out of her shoulder. With the room on fire and countless bodies around them, Darla's eyes rolled up in their sockets and she fell unconscious in Bader's arms.

"Darla!" Her sister cried. "No! Please…"

Bader grabbed a chair and threw it at the woman with the wand. Her wicked sorcery was interrupted, and the circle of elements she had created dissipated. It seemed the men who had imprisoned him – the "White Hats" as Bader has picked up from amidst the chaos- had managed to defend themselves yet again, for the air had cleared. However, Bader knew that the witch would soon recover and start again. Therefore he held Darla and dangled her on his shoulder. The vampire and the Asian dragon were starting to recover as well and they had to hurry.

"Get on," he growled at the little girl.

Darla's sister complied without hesitation. She climbed onto his back and held on tight to his shoulders. He then ran out of the great hall through a long corridor. He reached a door that led to several steps of stairs and knew that this was the exit. It would've been just that easy to escape if it weren't for a thin, short, bearded man who stood guard at the doorway. At his feet lay several charred corpses. *I can take him.*

The man threw fire at the gargoyle and the girls. Bader secured Darla on his right shoulder, while the sister held on tight to his back. He jumped into the air and the claws of his left hand pierced the ceilings. Pebbles fell to the sides as he dangled from the ceiling and growled at the bearded man. However, the man did not flinch nor budge. Bader then jumped on the short man's shoulder attempting to smash him into the ground. He was surprised to find that, as little and skinny as he was, the man was quite a tough nut to crack. A heat suddenly sizzled beneath his paws and he saw that the man's shoulders were ablaze. The scorching fire did not seem to affect the man who remained still. Bader fell to the ground on top of Darla and the girl crushing them. He wrapped his tail around the man's legs and pulled at them but the tiny man was not even effected.

The tiny man grinned.

"Now I know why gargoyles are extinct" he said with a heavy Arab accent

"Nice accent." Bader spat blood as he recognized the heavy Arab dialect.

The Jade Necklace

The grin changed back into a blank face. The little girl was unconscious next to Darla and they were all probably doomed.

"You mock me? May Allah take pity on you, freak." A fire ball formed in the Arab's hand and he threw it at Bader, hitting his shoulder. Catching fire, he leaped and threw himself on the tiny Arab setting him ablaze as well. In discord, the man had to move securing Bader's exit. The gargoyle rolled onto the ground, extinguishing the flames that licked at his flesh. Then, despite his sizzled skin, he grabbed both girls, placed them each on a different shoulder, and flew up the stairs and out of the flower shop until all three of them were high up in the air. His strength was about to falter but he had to fly onward to save them both. The night was his and he made use of the strength it still offered him. When he reached his mansion, he crashed in through the second story window and fell to the ground, with both girls by his sides. He morphed into his human self as he rolled onto his back in agonizing pain.

He was naked and barely breathing. He crawled helplessly on the ground through the shattered glass that further aggravated his agony till he reached the phone. He sent a text to Reed.

Help. Mansion.

He then passed out and entered a world of psychotic fantasies:

He was a little boy running around the fields on a summer day. He wore a knee length tunic which was fastened at the waist with a black belt. He ran around and lost himself in the midst of the tall grass. He knew that this was either a dream or memory, but could not wake up, nor had any control over his actions. He was five years old, a thousand years ago and his name was Robin.

"Robin! Where are you?" she called to him. *Agnes.*

She was the scullery maid of the castle and had taken it upon herself to raise him.

He sprinted towards her in laughter and once he had reached her she took him up in her arms and gave him her most saintly smile.

Agnes was a fair maiden of sixteen. Robin always liked to play with her golden hair. It soothed him. Her eyes were emerald green and her body had many curves. Many of the castle's tenants wished to bed her but she was under the protection of its Lord, so none dared. Robin never understood why Lord Alaric protected and treated Agnes differently from all the other maids. He did not understand that until it was too late to act.

She did not have to raise him, nor provide for him with the little amount of money she had. She did it anyway though, and for that, Bader had always been grateful. The castle he lived in was on a small island off the coast of England. No one in the present knew that the castle even existed or even knew of the very island it was built on. History washed away every memory of it and it had long been forgotten. Caleb, the most ferocious gargoyle to have ever roamed the lands of men at the time, made sure of that.

In spite of all of Caleb's atrocities, this was the one good thing he had ever done. His act protected the gargoyle species from being discovered by men, which spared him a lifetime of persecution.

Robin was born and raised in that very castle and life was good. The castle was heavily guarded by gargoyles, large monuments of beast by day and monstrous creatures by night. The gargoyles protected the island's tenants and maintained the rule of King Aldus over it. Few castles had their very own gargoyles for most only guarded the King's castle and the castles of the most prominent Lords. However, when needed, the King's decree would send gargoyles to defend whichever part of this small kingdom that needed their aid. In return for their services, gargoyles were offered security during the day time and cattle to feast on at night. Robin lived in one of such castles and had always felt safe during his childhood. Far away kings and armies feared the island and none dared raise arms against it.

Robin belonged to both worlds. He was a human raised by Agnes by day. But, come the night, he was the son of Caleb- Lord of the gargoyles- and, his Lady, Afra. At night, he was a little monster. Caleb was stronger and larger than any other gargoyle and the King himself had requested him to guard his own castle. Caleb, however, chose to protect Lord Alaric's city instead of King's. Caleb had hatched from his egg during the rule of Lord

Alaric's father in that very castle and the two were inseparable as children. When they were ten, Lord Alaric's father fell ill and died and it was their friendship that propelled Alaric down the path to true leadership. Caleb ensured the safety of the ten year old Lord Alaric as he ascended to his Lordship at such a young age and treated him like the younger brother he never had. Caleb loved him immensely and it was rumored that they could have been more than mere friends.

As for Robin, his secret was safe at first. No one knew that the child would turn to human by daylight and ever since he uttered his first words, he was taught by Agnes to keep his nature secret even from his father, Caleb. And so he did.... Until one day, when the truth of his human nature was revealed, all hell broke loose and Robin's world was shattered to a million pieces.

That part of the dream, Bader did not like and so he woke and returned to reality.

Chapter Seven: The Aftermath

It was early in the morning when Clara took up her regular seat in class. The teacher was going on and on about acids and bases but she couldn't care less. It wasn't like she was going to need this information during her medical career. There was the looming dread of the MCAT on the horizon but that wasn't until the second semester and she'd have plenty of time to review this kind of useless material by then.-It would be really funny if by the time she got into med school, she'd realize that she couldn't treat patients without a basic knowledge of acid base systems, but she doubted it. True, most material required for the MCAT had so little to do with Medicine, but who was she to argue with the system. She knew that the only road to success was to agree with your superiors, kiss ass and do as you're told no matter what. And that's what she planned to do.

As for the finals, she could always just ask Andrew or Widad to go over the orgy with her to make sure that she knew it all. *Hmmph that's a nice nickname for Organic Chemistry: Orgy. Oops I'm in Analytical Chem, focus Clara focus.*

She always found it useful to explain the material to others as it helped her assimilate most of it. What she found to be dreadful and an utter waste of time was the fact that she was forced to sit through lectures, where people who couldn't give a rat's ass about anything would be reading useless slides of material copied from textbooks. She knew she had to eventually go through all this material to get ahead but she hated being forced into attending a class. Others found classes useful but she never did and, as a young adult, couldn't for the life of her figure out why she should be treated like a school kid and be forced to sit through this charade.

She had greater concerns at the moment though.

Erick saw her do the unimaginable the night before. She was in disbelief about it herself. Could he be thinking about what had happened as well? Or was he all too consumed with his Creative Writing course? She knew he actually did want to become a writer someday and she respected him for it. Erick had registered for a premed program at first, like the rest of them, but after a full semester of biology and chemistry, he was fed up. He switched majors to English Literature and had gained Clara's respect ever since. He was a dreamer and dreamers are the ones who live happily ever after, she thought. She wondered if he was thinking about the other night, and whether he saw her in a new light: as his savior, his muse, his lady! She could think of nothing else. How on earth could she possibly possess such power? Was she an alien? A witch? Some descendant from an ancient line of Xena warrior princesses?

She was introduced to a new world and this both frightened and excited her. It mitigated her sense of worthlessness, in Erick's eyes at least, but illuminated the darker path she may have to walk to find out the truth about her origins.

Last night in the car, Erick brought up the subject. "Did you make that man slam into the wall? He said you had powers. What did he mean? What the hell happened?" He asked in a calm yet panicked tone as Clara realized that perhaps it was true: perhaps it was time to admit that she did have actual powers. It wasn't the first time she felt a surge of unordinary energy within her. She knew she cared deeply about Eric and maybe the thought of him getting hurt triggered some power within her. And perhaps, just perhaps, that power had been the reason why the man in black had come after her all those years ago. Perhaps the events of last night had been the catalyst that would help her find the truth about what happened to her parents and Yara. She thought that if she could tell him the full story, he might see her as being special. He might fall in love with her and they could live happily ever after. He could help her find those who killed her family and, together, they would be the heroes who bring forth the retribution.

"I don't know how I did that... It's never happened before," she said, adjusting her passenger seat so she'd be able to lean back.

"Well one thing's for sure, you're not only sexy and smart; now you're a super girl, too. We'd make a damn cool couple." He shifted in his seat and looked directly into her eyes. She couldn't help but wonder if he had finally come to see that she was the one who truly loved him. They truly had the potential to be an icon of love for others to look up to. It made sense in her mind because they had the same principals when it came to many things. They had been friends for so long and understood each other very well. They had even had the sex talk at some point and realized how attuned they could have been in bed. Could it be that her dreams were finally about to come true? Could it be that she was finally about to get her prince charming?

"I think I must have inherited something from… well the truth is… I'm actually adopted," she said before she gave him an account of what she had been through throughout her childhood. She told him of how she had been having dreams of a large winged beast that saved her from the burning house. She told him about how she woke up in a hospital in Lebanon with no ID or record, how she was sent to an orphanage until she was eventually welcomed into the arms of the Kfoury family, and how her new parents loved her like their own and treated her as they treated their own son, Youssef. But it still didn't erase the memories in her mind.

She expressed that she still believed her real family could be alive but that she had never been able to uncover any record that they ever existed.... That frightened her beyond anything. She told him about the man in black and that what they had just uncovered could be the key to finding her family again, or at least her sister who, she was almost certain, was alive.

"So the man who attacked us?" he asked.

"I don't know. Maybe he works for the man in black."

"You think he might know what happened to your family?"

"We'll have to find him again. Did you notice that we're both being awfully cool about this?"

"Maybe because we've seen too many movies," he said and they both laughed. "Try to do it again"

She honed her senses and focused on his shirt. She wanted to unbutton it with her mind to reveal the washboards abs that she could fry eggs on. She could not. Somehow, the power surge that flooded her insides earlier could not be ignited

"I can't. It must have happened because I thought you were going to get hurt," she replied.

"We'll figure it out. You did it once, you can do it again." He reassured her as he held her hand for a second then quickly pulled it away. Could that have been their moment? She soared above the clouds, for he had touched her the way lovers do.

But that was last night. Today, he might have had a change of heart after having slept on it.

When her class was dismissed, Clara quickly went out to the busy terrace in hopes of finding him. She went to the terrace that overlooked Beirut and managed to catch a glimpse of him straight below on the ground floor sitting at a round table with Grace-Marie, who was busy devouring a burger. Around her, students went about their normal daily lives, as if this day weren't special or different. Some ate their sandwiches, others studied relentlessly while a few had strange conversations about whether Haifa Wehbe is the hottest woman alive or not.

"Why were you in bad shape yesterday, babe? What's wrong?" She heard Grace-Marie ask in a loud voice.

Erick replied, which she could tell from his lips moving, but she couldn't hear what he said.

"You're such a girl," she said. This ticked him off and everyone began to stare as they began to argue. He was the sweetest man alive, the most open-minded man alive, but he was still a man, after all, and his ego was fragile. Grace-Marie had always been an attention seeker and she could always win any argument by simply raising her voice and embarrassing whoever she was arguing with. Clara never thought she would do that to Erick. She always thought that the stories she had heard him tell of their countless public break-ups were exaggerations from his part.

Erick mumbled something but seemed to be getting angry. He even stood up towards the end and waved his arm like a maestro.

"I'm not even gay for god's sakes," she shrieked. "Man! It was truth or dare, stop acting like a dumb cheesy faggot." Her voice got all squeaky as some of the guys laughed. Clara realized that they must have been talking about the kiss from the other night.

"Shut up Mary... Just don't... you kissed someone else in front of my face... I could never do that to you... if it were me, if I had kissed a guy, what would you do?" He asked. He finally raised his voice and Clara could hear the irritation in his tone very clearly. She wanted nothing other than to hug him, to kiss him, to make him feel better. She didn't agree with him, though: Grace-Marie did nothing wrong in her opinion, it was such silly fun. However, she would never have done that to him, had she been in Gracie's fake Louboutin shoes. She loved him too much and wanted every part of her to be his and his alone.

"I'd dump your ass," Gracie snapped. "But that's because you're a guy! It's different." She continued speaking and he began to look impatient.

"I have to go. Grow up." He walked away from her.

"You'll be back; you're too much of a sissy to leave me…" she yelled as she walked the other way, still taking bites out of her burger.

It was time for her class with Professor Montgomery and Clara needed to hurry there. She would just have to talk to Erick later. She did make it in the nick of time but Andrew had been late as usual. He had two classes with the she-demon and knew better than to be late. Clara, on the other hand, was luckier since she had just one. She took a seat.

"I'm sorry I cannot allow you to enter. You're ten minutes late," Professor Jennifer Montgomery said. She was a tall, thin, middle-aged woman. Hidden features of a forgotten beauty lingered behind her glasses.

"I'm sorry, it won't happen again. I promise," Andrew assured her with a smile as he walked into the room casually.

"Are you aware that you're wasting the time of those who came here to learn?" she argued. She stood up and walked to the door at the back of the room, opened it, and waited by its side with the stillness of stone.

"I am here to learn," he argued back in a shy tone. *OH OH, she's gonna eat him alive.*

"Are you done? Will you please close the door on your way out?" He headed for the door but before he could exit, she placed her hand on his shoulder. "Oh, and Mister Kozah, try to drop the course at your earliest convenience please," she said with the calmest voice.

As Andrew left the class, Professor Montgomery shut the door and continued her lecture on her way back to her seat, as if nothing had happened. *She's going to force him to drop her classes…charmouta! Dammit.*

****

During lunch, Erick and Clara met in the cafeteria. It was just the two of them this time, and she was in bliss. He would tell her that he's considering a break up from Gracie. They would discuss her special powers. He would come to love her in time.

 The cafeteria had been extremely crowded but she felt as if it were only the two of them. It was as though the rest of the world had ceased to exist. Erick was the kind of guy that could always make her feel special!

"So what happened to you? You look like a train wreck."

She hoped he'd give her the news of his break up.

"It's Mary. We had a fight," he said as he looked down. "You saw how she kissed Carmen."

Clara struggled with whether or not to tell him what she really thought of the matter.

"Erick, it was just a game. And you were there. So, technically… it's not that much of a big deal" she tried to explain.

"She disrespected me in front of everyone," he said angrily.

"Erick…" she tried to interject.

"I mean, when you're in a serious relationship with someone, you're not supposed to kiss other people. Period."

"Every couple makes their own rules for their relationship. Maybe you guys haven't established your own," she said feeling as if she had swallowed mud. She didn't want to disagree with him but she couldn't help it.

"She knows how I feel about this stuff. I made it clear to her that it pisses me off if she were to ever do such a thing."

"If you guys talked about this before, it's a different deal but if you haven't then there's nothing wrong with what she did... for now."

"Man, I don't know... let's just drop the subject," he said but Clara was too eager to find out if he would think of breaking up.

"What are you going to do?"

"I don't know... I love her; I just don't know how to work things out. It's not the first time she's disappointed me this much."

"You'll figure things out."

Carmen walked into the cafeteria and headed to sit with her friend Shereen. *Thank God she didn't sit with us.* Carmen and Shereen had known each other from the sixth grade and they've been friends ever since. The stories of how they would get in trouble at school were part of the horror that Carmen had inflicted on Clara when she first became her roommate. Come the spring semester, she'll never have to suffer through the retellings of those adventures again since she was going to request a transfer to another room.

Shereen was a fair skinned blonde with blue eyes and humongous breasts that everyone mistook for implants, and she was the Queen of the three bitches otherwise known as Shereen, Carmen and Grace-Marie.

"Hey, Shereen, I feel really bad, I think Clara is really mad at me," said Carmen.

I'm right behind you Dumbo. Erick continued to eat his salad as Clara eavesdropped on Shereen and Carmen's conversation.

"Do you think I would look good as a redhead?" Asked Shireen. *Could you get any shallower?*

"Yes you would. So we were playing truth or dare at the party and I kissed her friend's…"

Aren't they really far away? Maybe I have super hearing now too.

"Erick? Can you hear what Carmen is saying?" Erick looked around and Clara realized that Carmen was sitting at the very edge of the cafeteria with her back turned to them. The cafeteria was overflowing with people, and people meant noise! It was impossible to overhear that conversation especially that she wasn't even remotely interested in those girls' lives!

"No, why?"

"I think I have super hearing or something," she said, half joking, half serious.

Erick choked on his water and coughed up a laugh.

"I'm thinking of going brunette" continued Shereen. "I think it suits my style more you know?"

"Ok, good for you. So the point is..." Carmen spoke as Shireen fixed her makeup as she checked herself out with her portable mirror. "Are you listening to anything I'm saying?"

"What?" Shireen asked innocently. "You're so cute when you're upset."

"Hello! Clara's...!"

"Who's Clara?"

The Jade Necklace

"My roommate!"

"Yeah, honey-bunny, go on... anyway, so I had a date with a billionaire and..."

"Do you even care about what's going on with me?"

"Of course I do, honey-bunny... so anyways... he spent so much money... and you cannot believe his house, I had an orgasm just from looking..."

"You're a bitch... you know that?" Carmen snapped.

"I'm leaving... I'm late for class. Bye babe." Shireen snapped her mirror shut, placed it in her black Prada and moseyed away.

Poor Carmen.

"Hello! Clara?" Erick's voice anchored her to this reality. She had been gone for a few minutes, listening in on the girls' conversation. *My powers are cool.*

"Let's walk out," he said.

They both walked down the hall and she explained to him how she managed to hear the entire conversation very clearly.

"Okay, so what is that guy saying?" He pointed to a guy standing far away at the end of the hallway talking on the phone.

"I don't know. I can't control it..."

She spotted Andrew innocently drinking his Pepsi and walking right past the guy on the phone, heading towards them with a smile on his face.

"Don't say anything in front of Andrew."

It was then that Marc, the big fat bully, headed towards their friend and she knew that there was going to be trouble.

"What's up, faggy?" Marc smirked as he pushed Andrew into the wall and spilled his coke all over Andrew's shirt.

"What the hell?" Andrew panicked.

"Andy, how does it feel like to have a thick cock rammed up your hole?" Marc joked when he was grabbed by Erick and shoved away. Andrew looked at his savior in gratitude. *I love that guy.*

"Stay away from him," Erick said. He threw Marc head first in the trash bin. Clara rushed to Andrew's side.

The Jade Necklace

"You okay?" she asked.

"Whatever!" Andrew quickly got up and rushed away.

Clara knew in her heart that Andrew was most likely to be gay and his denial was not healthy. She knew that Andrew must have been really scared of what he was... He might have even felt self-loathing or guilt. She didn't know what to do. She couldn't reveal her suspicions because that could do more damage and she didn't want to put him on the spot. The best way, she thought, was to show him how accepting of homosexuals she was and wait for him to feel safe enough to reveal himself to her. At the end of the day, she wasn't even sure if he was gay to begin with. A lot of the guys she knew were metrosexual, and Andrew could easily fall into that category. But she wasn't going to ask him and ruin a perfectly good friendship.

Later in the day, when her classes were finished, Clara found herself knocking on Widad's door. They were supposed to sign up for the MCAT from Widad's apartment since she had the fastest internet connection and Lebanon lagged behind civilized nations in that field.

When Widad opened, Clara was surprised at the fright that had taken hold of Fatima's eyes. Her body was shaking like a leaf. She was breathless and her face was pale. She was afraid to move. Every muscle of her body fidgeted and danced all on its own as though she had a terminal stage of Parkinson's. Fatima noticed that the girls were watching her and froze. Her legs still moved like little ducklings but for the most part her upper body was still.

"Fatima, what's wrong? It's just a show honey and it's... well, haven't you watched Buffy before?" asked Widad.

"I just got it on DVD and I need to go to the bathroom! And no, I haven't seen it before... it's amazing." Fatima said in a shaking voice.

"Then, go!" Widad said.

"I want to see what happens. She just turned into a man!" Fatima was surprised. She pointed at the screen.

"I love Alyson Hannigan." Clara joined in.

"She was on *How I Met Your Mother*, too. I love her! Oh my God. Now I have to rewind! Stop talking, you guys!" Fatima said.

"It's a DVD. You can pause it." Clara laughed.

Fatima was a brown haired girl who obsessively followed any TV series she could find. She wasn't the most sociable of girls but managed to maintain a healthy friendship with Widad. Her darker skin tone gave her an exotic appeal but she didn't take advantage of it to get boys. She was one of the biggest nerds the university had ever seen but she was easily wanted by most of the boys. *Why doesn't anyone want me?*

"Let's go to your room," Clara said to Widad.

But before they entered Widad's bedroom, Clara felt extremely light headed. She fell to the ground and suddenly saw the outside of Grace-Marie's house. Was she there? Was she dreaming? Was this some form of astral projection?

Erick was in his car, waiting for Grace to come out. After making him wait for twenty minutes which to Clara seemed like a decade, the royal lady came out of the building and slowly strolled to the car. Gracie entered the car armed by an emotionless face.

"What do you want?" she asked slowly articulating her words.

"Are you going to do it again?" He inquired, still angered by her behavior.

"It was just a kiss. It didn't mean anything."

Liar! Liar! Wasn't I on her side a few hours ago?

Clara wondered what was happening to her body during that time. Widad must have been extremely worried but she couldn't go back; she needed to know what would happen.

"Then why don't we break up so you can kiss whoever you want?"

"I don't want to break up. But I don't want to be tied down; that's all. I'm not a relationship kind of gal but I'm doing this for you…"

"Oh thank you, your highness for getting off Your throne for me."

"I changed my life for you!"

"Yes, you stopped banging three guys a day!"

"Fuck you!" she argued.

"My girlfriend is a hoe who can't commit!"

"That has nothing to do with... wake up Erick! Kissing someone or fucking someone means nothing! It's just fun and has nothing to do with how I feel about you... But I'm not doing that for *you*, to make *you* happy," she replied. "I love *you*."

"Then never make out with anyone again... and never go partying with Shereen and Carmen again! You can be friends with them but I... I don't... could you please just...? You have a history of getting drunk and making out with random guys... I just don't want to..."

"You don't trust me?"

"I don't trust them... I don't trust..."

"Fine. I won't go to her parties anymore. Happy?"

"Thank you."

"Can you be kissing me now?" She asked right before he planted a kiss on her lips.

When she got out of the car, she waved goodbye and sent him an air kiss. He drove off and she dialed Shereen's number. *You bitch.*

"Hey guess what, we made up."

"I just fucked that billionaire I dated. He thought I was a prostitute and left me some cash on the desk. What a freak!" *How can I hear what the Queen devil is saying through the phone?*

"When I talk you don't interrupt chica!" Grace-Marie exclaimed. "So he just wants me to stop kissing random people and partying with you."

"What? Are you crazy? There's this really cool after-party in two weeks… everyone who is anyone is going to be there… we have to be there…. Carmen is in!"

"Relax girlfriend… I'll just lay low for a couple of weeks. He'll come around."

"You bet he will. I'd like to get a ring around my finger, too." Shereen said.

"It's called love; you can Google it," Gracie replied.

"Why are you still with him? He's such a loser," Shereen asked.

"Because... I love him," she explained.

Clara wondered if Grace-Marie actually did feel something for Erick but brushed it off.

It was then that she saw her old burning house clearly exactly where Gracie's building had stood. She saw a winged beast twice the size of a normal man break through the window and come out carrying a young unconscious Clara in his arms only to fly away into the black sky. *I must be very powerful. I need to find the man with the yellow eyes!!* He could be the lead she had been looking forward to dig into her family's fate, she thought as she heard a soft, rattling noise. A fog began to emerge from the north of where she stood, just as the rattling increased in pitch. A whisper, carried by the wind, shrieked as it reached her ears: "Arisha."

A monster stepped out of the fog but Clara dared not move. *This isn't real.* He had pale, white skin, red eyes, and the face of a man wearied by more than a thousand years of age: the face of a living corpse. The monster was strangely agile and as it made its way towards her, she turned away from him to run.

But suddenly, she found herself standing in a meadow where a young boy, who couldn't be older than fifteen, smiled at her. He had hazel eyes that changed to black. They became black holes, eternal pits of despair. "My love," he said just as her sharp teeth bit her lower lip, almost unconsciously. She heard his heartbeat, the ants treading on the soil, the blood coursing through his veins, the rustling of leaves in the wind. He smelled good and she wanted to have him. The jade necklace was still around her neck but she was strangely dressed in a green dress like an ancient princess. The boy approached her but was taken aback when she smiled. Her sharp canines brushed against her lips and she knew what she was. She dug her teeth deep into his neck and drank him. His heart was beginning to slow down, when she saw a man dressed in black standing behind her boy. She let him go, his body falling to the ground. She could not discern the features of the man in black. He wore a black hat, a long black coat, black pants and black shoes.

"You are an abomination," he said in an almost demonic voice. A chill went through her and she woke up in Widad's bed.

"Are you Okay? I brought you *Mazaher*." Widad said nervously. Fatima was there as well, sitting at the foot of the bed. Clara got up and, without a word to Widad or Fatima, walked out. She had developed three powers so far that she could not control: astral projection or the power of visions – she wasn't sure which - telekinesis and strong hearing. She couldn't control any of them but was certain that if she were to run into Lex, the attacker from the other night, again she would get the hang of at least her telekinesis.

She walked the empty streets alone thinking of the meaning of her vision. The winged monster, the white faced corpse and the man in black. What did they mean? Why was she seeing the past and why did the man in black call her an abomination. Engulfed in her thoughts, she did not notice when a car parked right next to her. She heard a honk and turned to see that it was Erick.

"Clara? What are you up to?" He asked.

"I... I'm going home," she lied.

"Dorm gate will be closed by the time you get there. I can drive you."

"No... It's okay; I want to walk."

"He's not going to attack you again, Clara. He knows what you're capable of now," Erick reasoned. He could read her mind so well. He knew that she wanted to be attacked by Lex so she could defeat and question him. People who know each other that well are the best of lovers and she loved him. Why couldn't he love her back?

"Which makes me a better target. He knows what I am, and if he was one of those men who hurt my parents, he's going to come after me again."

"In that case, he'll know where to find you. You don't have to walk down the street on your own at night."

"I have to know! What happened to my parents, my sister? She was having a sleep-over that night and the police report stated that she never even existed! They said that there was no family living in that house! There was no one living there when it burned down! The only thing they said they found in there was the burnt body of a six-year-old girl who had snuck in at night and accidentally set fire to the house! I need to find them, Erick! They faked my death! I know it! They were trying to protect me!" Clara kept trying to explain as the tears flooded her face. He stepped out of the car and tucked her deeply in his arms. She sobbed quietly on his shoulder, a brief moment of peace.

"Then I'll stay with you. I don't want you to get hurt. I love you," he said.

Clara was overwhelmed with the desire to kiss him but managed to contain herself. She didn't want to make a fool out of herself.

"So what happened with Mary?" she asked, eagerly hoping he would say that he broke up with Gracie, that his heart belonged to her, Clara, and her alone. She wanted him to say that she is his true soul mate and that he longed to be with her. She wanted to hear that her touch gave him goose bumps and that the idea of kissing her filled his stomach with butterflies. She wanted him to want her! She wanted to be his and his alone. But her vision- or astral projection, whatever that was- experience had told her otherwise.

"I don't know. We had a fight; it'll pass... I just... nothing... forget it."

"What is it? Tell me. Tell me."

"I almost told her that I wish she could be more like you, that I wish I were dating you But that would've hurt her. So... yeah."

"We wouldn't want her to get hurt," Clara said, disappointed.

They wandered in the empty street together.

The Jade Necklace

Chapter Eight: The lone Wolf

Bader slowly opened his eyes. He could tell that he was in his chambers at Reed's mansion, for in spite of the vague images rushing to his head, he could put the pieces together. The room was quite large but all too empty. It merely consisted of the essentials, just as he had wished. It had a master bed by the window, the view from which was the most beautiful and sophisticated garden one could ever dream of. Beside the bed of silk sheets, there was a night table upon which there was an old-fashioned lamp. The floor was covered with Persian carpets and a chandelier was hung from the ceiling. Across the room were a few couches around a large wooden table - that was the meeting room. By the door stood a small fridge that contained nothing but water and beer, his favorite drink.

She was in the room with him; he could see her hazy face but did not utter her name.

"He's awake," it was Reed. The figures were a haze but he could tell who was who. Darla had the long hair and Reed was the short man with four eyes.

Reed had come to his rescue more than once. That man had never let him down and Bader appreciated having him as the closest thing to a friend. He had held Reed on the day he was born, and he knew him well. Reed could have been a younger brother but Bader could not let himself care for others. He mostly treated him as a mere employee and attempted to avoid all forms of bonding activities with the man. He was immortal, the Reeds were not. He had once loved Marcus Reed's great, great grandfather, Cain. They had gone by a different last name then, and if it weren't for Bader their blood-line would have been extinguished. He helped Cain come to power and came to love him with all his heart, but fate took him too soon. But not before Bader formed an everlasting bond with the Reeds, intertwining his fate to theirs forever.

The figure alluding to Darla approached him and sat by his side. Her expression changed into what he assumed was a smile. A sound of laughter, all too familiar, haunted him. It was the laughter of the boy he once was. He drifted off into yet another deep sleep.

He was Robin again, running around the castle. He climbed the flight of stairs that led to the highest tower and watched his gargoyle family sleeping. The gargoyles had nested at the edge of a large terrace from which one could see far away distances. But up on high, on the highest tower, Caleb and Afra stood in their statue forms next to one another. They were double the size of the men he'd spend his days observing. A gargoyle's fist could easily be twice the size of a man's. His father could protect him from anyone who dared lay a finger on him and that could make any little boy feel secure. Caleb was the largest of all the gargoyles. Towering over his subjects, Caleb stood tall arching his back forward. His clawed hands extended before him as if he were about to strike at someone. "The warrior's sleep," Robin called it. His father's face, was monstrous and square. He seemed to stare out into the horizon as if waiting for the right moment to fly into battle.

Robin's eyes caught the lady Afra's which were looking down at the ground. She wasn't as large as his father and stood slightly hunched and let down. It seemed to Robin that her oval face expressed such sorrow. She was considered a great beauty among gargoyles, even as she slumbered. From up there, Robin could see the whole countryside. He used to spend hours clinging on to Caleb's stony back watching peasants plow the fields like little ants, rivers on their journey to the sea, and far off mountains of ice. It was a beautiful country – at least, that was how he remembered it. He used to dream of going to places beyond the horizon and having adventures: saving a princess from a dragon or fighting a Cyclops. He would be a hero. That wasn't possible though; as a boy, he could not go far, and as a gargoyle, he was not allowed to fly off on his own. For now, he had to be content with just being a boy who is very much loved by all.

By day, the little boy, Robin, was the bastard son of Agnes the scullery maid. He was taught by both his Lady Mother and Agnes to lie, especially to his father about his human side. Agnes had told him that he was special and different from all the others. If anyone were to find out that he was a day walker, then both gargoyles and humans would want to hurt him.

Robin loved his father Caleb very much. Every night when he would turn into his true self, he would fly off into distant places with Caleb who would teach him how to hunt, fight and what it meant to be the guardians of their castles. Caleb seldom laughed but Robin always managed to get to him. The one thing Robin was sure of was the love that his father bore for him and he wanted to tell him about his secret more than anything in the whole world. He knew his father would love him unconditionally and wouldn't care that he was different. However, he feared his mother's wrath and, therefore, could not speak up. His mother was one of the most vicious gargoyles there was, and Robin had seen her tear apart large men who tried to harm Lord Alaric, the lord of the castle where they had resided. Robin didn't want to make her cross with him, so he held his tongue and enjoyed the nights he had with his family, for it was during the night when he would be his true self, the son of Lord Caleb, strongest and fairest of all the gargoyles.

A happy memory or a happier era, but that was all it was. Time moves forward and waits for no one and in his heart, Bader knew that Robin died long ago. The sweet young man that he was, died when Aurora was taken from him and there was no going back.

When Bader woke up at last, it was dark outside. He instantly sprung to his feet and morphed into his monstrous self. He was fully energized and promptly flew out the window breaking it on the way out. *Reed will take care of that.*

He could imagine the look on Reed's face when he'd walk in to see the covers on the floor next to shards of glass. The Reeds, after all, had no stay-in servants - they merely hired help for a few hours a day, something Bader had requested. He didn't want to have to eat the help if they unearthed his secret. No matter, the maid would clean up the mess the next day and Reed will come up with a cover story.

He was strong again, his skin was unscathed, his mind wide open and his eyes as predatory as ever. A gargoyle heals fast, but a gargoyle also needs to feed. Feeding on humans wasn't compulsory but it was, in fact, the meal that made him the strongest. He recalled the first time he had met Reed's ancestor, Cain. Wounded in a fight against mighty gargoyles, Robin had fallen into a lake. Cain was a mere fisherman at the time. When he pulled Robin out of the water, he was not afraid simply because what he had found was a wounded man. He took him to his small cabin and nursed him back to health in secret. Cain lived with his elderly mother, and in spite of being almost thirty years of age, had still not been able to get married. When the strange man he had found regained his health, Cain's life changed for the better as he learned of the man's dark secret... To Cain, to Reed, to Aurora and Darla, even Darla's kid sister, Bader must have been some hero. But he knew what he truly was. He was a monster.

He spotted his next victim like an eagle from the sky: a tall muscular man, no not a man, a vampire, roaming the dark streets in search of a victim to feed on. *You're going to pay for what the blond pussy did.* The vampire he had faced earlier was stronger than most and he wasn't likely to run into him any time soon. Bader needed to take out his frustration on someone: who better than another weaker vampire.

Bader dove down from the skies and landed on top of the vampire, grabbed him by the shoulders with his hind paws, and flew up into the heights. The vampire bit his leg and Bader growled in fury. He grabbed the vampire by his hair and lifted him up to eye level. He placed his one hand on the vampire's shoulder for support right before he tore the head from the body with the other. He let the head fall down and devoured the body quickly, before it aged. He did not manage to eat it whole for it had turned to dust. But the torso was enough to quench his appetite. *Vampires taste good.*

Bader flew back to the mansion, back into his bedroom as the sun dawned on the world. He changed back to a man. He put on his trousers and walked out of the room shirtless. He walked down the long corridor of fancy Persian rugs until he reached the glass ball stairs. He headed down then walked into the kitchen where Reed and Darla were laughing as they ate cheesecake. The little girl was there, too, though he didn't see her at first.

"By all means, don't let me interrupt," Bader spoke coldly as he sat beside them at the round table at the center of the kitchen.

"Glad you're doing well, boss man." Reed smiled.

"If he hadn't found us in time, I think we would've died ... I wanted to say that I'm..." she swallowed. "I mean... I'm sorry for..." said Darla timidly.

"Save it," Bader interrupted.

"Very well, I'll be out of your hair in no time." She set her fork on the table, her eyes full of the unsaid. The chair scraped against the floor as she stood up. Darla walked away angrily and went up the stairs. "Annabelle!" she called out to the fifteen year old who quickly left the kitchen and trailed behind her sister.

"What was that for, boss man?" Reed commented, cleaning his glasses.

He could tell Reed was upset. But those two words had come out inadvertently. He did not mean to push her away but he had done enough for her already and couldn't risk having another friend. He didn't want to feel the sting of loss again.

"Where's Sera?" He tried to calmly change the subject ignoring the growing concern for the girl who began to enter his heart. If he were to protect the girl, he'd have to religiously commit to his cannibalistic diet. A gargoyle's at his strongest when he feasts on the raw flesh of the living, especially humans or mages. He wouldn't mind that, but he would protect her to what end? All mortals die sooner or later. If he were to protect her from the witch and those assailants, she could die of cancer the next year or get hit by a car the next day. Life was worthless.

Reed explained that his wife had taken their two children, Steven and Jane, to France on vacation and he had the mansion all to himself. He did not fail to remind Bader that no member of his family knew of his secret and none will until Steven, his eldest son, comes of age. When Bader was about to retire, Reed insisted that he should go after the girl. "She'll be easy prey without you," he said.

It was all too true; those men were not to be trifled with. Even he barely managed to escape and he was a *gargoyle*! The girl was surely strong and had the power of sight but she could not hope to stand up to them when they come after her. However, he was no hero and there was nothing he could do for her. *She's on her own.*

Jad El Khoury

Chapter Nine: Darla

Bader left the house and sat on a small swing that was hidden in the shadow at the very edge of the garden of flowers and roses. Night had fallen but he hadn't changed, he was calm. Darla still hadn't left; Reed had talked her into staying till the next day and Bader chose not to argue. He kicked his feet off the ground and the swing moved slightly backwards then forward. A soft gust of wind caressed his face and glided over his spiky black hair. Reed didn't like his new haircut, but he couldn't care less.

If he were to help the girl, he would put his own life in danger; but if he were to let her go, then she would wind up dead within a heartbeat. Bader did not harm the innocent, sure, but he never intended to protect them either. He wasn't a hero! *I don't want to be a fucking hero*! But wouldn't letting that girl die be the equivalent of killing her himself? He would be the one who condemns her to die. He looked up and saw her through her bedroom window. She had changed out of the clothes she had on a few days ago when they were attacked. She appeared more beautiful than ever under the moonlight. *I should tap that one more time.* She wore a white silky dress that made her all too radiating. His heart beats were becoming rapid and he suddenly realized that he couldn't let her go.

Annabelle, the sister, was not in the room. They had probably agreed with Reed's suggestion, hoping that if they stayed long enough, Bader would ask them to stay. He knew they wanted to stay, needed to stay.

She is the only person that he could ever find to be more of a freak than he was. She is a mage that cannot be categorized into any of the four elements her kind are born into. She was hunted for what she is and she believed that there was some good left in him. He could not send her off to meet a painful death. His feet anchored the swing in place and as he stood up he unbuttoned his shirt and took off his trousers and shoes. He was in a dark spot of the garden and no one could see him. Within moments, he doubled in size, his skin hardened and greyed, his eyes glowed bloody red and his features turned coarse.

He flew to her window but did not land. He beat his wings in mid-air until she noticed him.

After an awkward moment of silence, Bader extended his hand to Darla who strangely enough opened the window and extended her arm. He took her hand and, seconds later, she was in Bader's arms and he rose into the night's sky.

As they soared Darla looked down upon the city. He could tell that she was not scared, even though any person would be. He hoped that the girl would feel safe and that by having a monstrous creature by her side, no one would dare lift a finger at her. It seemed like their speed was accelerating just as Darla closed her eyes, her breath deepening. Opening her eyes again, they shared a most wondrous view. All of the beautiful colors melted into each other - city lights, stars, moon, the glow of her eyes, an airplane far above- in a most striking abstract form that neither of them could decipher. He couldn't help but wonder what was it that drew him towards this girl? He did not have time to process his thoughts coherently for they had reached their destination. They landed upon a tall building at the Front de Seine and they could see the whole city including the Eiffel tower.

They were quiet for some time until he asked her why those men were after her and her companions.

"I'm a phoenix."

She went on to explain that a phoenix is a mage that is born to the fifth element which is a combination of all four. A phoenix is fire for it is a creature of the flame, is wind for it can fly, is earth for it turns to ashes when it dies, and is water because a phoenix- much like water- represents life: it is always reborn. This renders the phoenix capable of accessing any kind of abilities that any mage that walks this earth can possess. Nobody knows much about the existence of this symbol, as it was extinct for millennia. The phoenixes were gone for unknown reasons and they were born again for a mysterious purpose. All that she knew was that Jonathan, who had the element of wind, was on a self-proclaimed mission to eradicate all phoenixes from existence. Jonathan was all too powerful. Whenever he is in proximity to a mage, he can use their powers against them. In addition to this, he had the sight and could harness the ability to foresee the future better than anyone, to dream walk, even to astral project and monitor people. Jonathan was also capable of some form of mind control, which he could exert on the weak. He was, by all means, a formidable foe.

The organization to which she belonged was known as the Brotherhood of the Dawn. It had existed for thousands of years across all cultures and in various forms. Its purpose was to provide mages with the proper guidance and protection in order to ensure that they remain at the side of Good. They are meant to safeguard all human and mage life on earth in the face of the evil as well as other nocturnal creatures.

The Brotherhood was led by a council of four of the most powerful mages that the world has come to know. One representing each element. Had the council of four been at the London headquarters, Darla believed, they would have been more than capable of stopping Jonathan. Unfortunately, all four haven't been seen in over three years. They had gone into a trance, a form of inner spiritual retreat to find answers concerning the return of the phoenixes, and their physical bodies were heavily guarded at an unknown location.

Darla hadn't always lived with the brotherhood. As children, she and Annabelle were raised in a family that she refused to speak of. Bader could tell from the tone of her voice when she spoke about it that it was probably an abusive household but didn't want to ask too much. He didn't wish to take her back to a painful past. Annabelle and Darla were then taken from their home, from their family by the brotherhood. They taught Darla how to use her abilities and she eventually decided to give back by training a new generation of mages alongside her day job as an executive assistant. She was different from those she trained and those around her, however, because she was born a phoenix. Unfortunately, she had no idea what that meant.

"So, you're a freak," he commented coldly.

She turned away from him towards the Seine. He knew he had hurt her feelings. He approached her and, as he morphed into his naked human self, he took her in his arms.

"From one freak to another, I promise I won't let anything bad happen to you."

She turned around to face him. Her skin was cold, her eyes wide open and her fingers shaking. Was she shaking because of him or the cold? He did not know. His lips found hers and they kissed.

"Thank you."

She gave him a sweet smile as her eyes looked down onto his flaccid organ.

"We should get back now," he said.

"I'm not in a hurry."

She gave him a wicked smile and his growing boner knew what she wanted. She raised her hands and slowly removed her dress. Her firm breasts and the erect nipples called out to him. They were very pink and small and he wanted nothing more than to savor them.

He grabbed one of her breasts with his right hand and slowly bent down towards it. He felt her shivering in his arms and looked up into her eyes before he suckled on the pink piece of heaven. He ravished it so hard that she moaned loudly into his ears holding on to his head with both arms. Her thighs found their way around his waist and he carried her with ease. His left hand grabbed her ass tight, spanking it till he left a reddened bruise. By then he had gotten too stiff to think. His ear was in her mouth and she bit at his lobe, and her tongue massaged his neck and his eyes rolled back in their sockets. She was holding on to him tightly as if begging for power. As he moved to the other nipple drawing a line with his tongue in between both, his middle finger found its way inside her wetness. It was warm down there, too warm, and he felt an urge to taste her but decided that it could wait. The grasp around his finger was too tight and he could only imagine how hard it would squeeze his cock once he shoved it inside her. As his middle finger throbbed into her vagina, his thumb caressed her engorged clitoris and his pinkie went up her ass. She moaned in ecstasy begging him not to stop. He hadn't felt so attracted to a woman in many many years. This wasn't a mere sexual encounter, this was something new. He wanted to be inside her, to be part of her. He wanted to merge with her into one and so he did.

He laid her on her back and mounted her. She grabbed his hair as his thighs moved between her legs and they both moaned in ecstasy when they came together after three throbs. *I came too quickly, can't get enough of her.*

He rolled off of her and her head sought refuge on his chest. She buried it deep into his pecks as an ostrich would bury its head in the sand. It felt good. He made her feel safe and protected in his arms and, for the first time in all those years, he actually liked it.

After a while, she put her white dress back on and as he morphed into his bestial self, they took off and headed back to the mansion. The flight was serene this time. He took the time to get back home and they observed the city that was under them. They quietly landed in her bedroom. And as he was about to excuse himself, she stopped him. Annabelle was sleeping on the bed and did not wake up.

"Can you... can you hold me tonight?" They walked out of her bedroom and headed to his.

She was like him. She had a humane side as well but was too afraid to show it. Her sentiment is reemerging just as he felt himself begin to yearn as well, and that is what made her so special to him. They slept next to one another, curled up in each other's arms in perfect serenity.

Chapter Ten: Heart of Darkness

In the black of night, his very soul belonged to her. Not that it didn't during the day, but night was the time when the vow they made to one another came back to haunt him. Near the meadows, Robin, the wet nurse's boy, had professed his undying love to Aurora, Princess of Amador. Her smile that day had been the most beautiful thing he had ever seen in his entire life. Her jade eyes glowed brighter than her jade necklace and he knew then and there that she was his forever. He had professed his love to his princess, her golden hair bathing in the holy sun that they had worshipped.

Her blushing cheeks alluded to her feelings but she dared not open her mouth. His hand found hers and she did not move. Her small pink fingers were serene within his grasp and in her oval eyes he saw himself smile. Through the lens of love, he saw that he was a young lad of fifteen, tall for his age and well built. The wind blew into his black soft hair and it made her smile. Her blonde locks were obscuring her face as they fluttered in the wind but then she did the sweetest thing. With her hand, she grabbed on to a lock of black hair and intertwined it with her golden locks. Together they were a perfect mixture of earth and gold, heaven and life, a lover and his muse! She laughed gleefully and Robin knew that he would never love another.

But fate had a different plan in store for the young lovers.

"Princess! Princess Aurora." Her handmaiden, Lisbeth, had come to ruin their moment. The princess hadn't confessed anything she felt towards him, but her smile was enough.

She turned around and looked at the regal castle and the handmaiden skipping towards them. "I'm coming!" She called out.

The princess ran through the fields, the wind in her hair, and reached Lisbeth who could barely walk on the soil without constantly tripping.

"What were you doing there, my princess?"

"We were just talking…"

"But he's a … he's a…"

"A person." The princess skipped towards the castle and the handmaiden struggled to keep up. When she got as far away as she could from Lisbeth, Aurora turned around as if to check what had taken the handmaiden so long. He knew that, in fact, her green eyes were fixed upon him. She was too far away and he could not be certain but in his heart, he knew that the smile was meant for him. Robin couldn't help but smile.

Bader awoke from his sleep of memories and willed them into his subconscious. He didn't need his humanity creeping back in. It was still dark and Darla lay next to him in bed. Her head rested on his chest as though it were a feathery pillow. She seemed to be having peaceful dreams. The moment he tried to get up, she opened her eyes.

"Where to?"

"I never told you where I come from," he said as he changed into a gargoyle.

"You're a good man; that's all I need to know." She sat up straight in bed, her auburn locks covering one of her bare breasts, the other plump and firm in its place.

"I'm not."

She got up and walked towards him planting a soft kiss on his grey monstrous cheek.

"You saved my life when you had no reason to. We've all been touched by darkness at one point or another, but you're... You're my hero, Bader."

My soul belongs to the darkness and my heart to the night. He was neither a man nor a hero. He couldn't be what she wanted. But with Darla, his heart felt warm. Yes, he was no hero but was going to protect both her and Annabelle. He didn't love her, maybe, but he did care for her.

"Don't go saying I love you now." He smiled wickedly and morphed back into a man. He was looking forward to a quick hunt before sunrise but as the rays crept in through the windows, he realized that he was too late. The sun was rising and with it his ability to change would be none existent.

"I'm not that kind of girl." She laughed. "Let's make breakfast for Annabelle and Marcus."

"Don't call him Marcus."

"Why? Are you afraid of humanizing him?" She laughed.

"Let's go."

"By the way, I would like to know something," she said as she stepped into the bathroom, keeping the door open. He followed and stood by the door as she opened the tap water and washed her face.

"How come you can turn into a man? From what I read, gargoyles turn to stone during the day. Now unless the books are wrong, which they could be since there hasn't been a gargoyle for over a thousand years..."

He just walked away. He was going to protect her but that didn't mean he had to open up to her and share the misery that was his past.

A long time ago, he learned what he was the hard way, he learned why he was different and he did not want to relive that anguish. In the kingdom of Amador, King Anais had come to rule peacefully for many years and the gargoyles had graced him with their loyalty and protection in return for his insurance of their survival during the sunlight hours. That all changed because of young Robin, and a war between humanity and gargoyles was waged, one that brought the extinction of the gargoyles and the end of Amador.

Later, in the kitchen, the four companions had bacon and eggs together while making plans for the near future. Bader was going to buy another mansion near where Reed lived and he was going to move Darla and Annabelle there so they could stay safe after he hunts down Jonathan. He wasn't planning on living with them but he would come and visit from time to time and would make sure that Reed and Sera would befriend and watch over the girls when he's gone. He wasn't a monogamous man, after all, and did not want any sort of commitment or any flat mates, even if the "flat" was in the form of a giant mansion. They planned for Annabelle to go to a private school around the area so that Darla could keep an eye on her. She could further develop her abilities at the mansion under Darla's guidance and then, at some point, they would be able to protect themselves should someone else attack them. Annabelle possessed the sign of Earth and therefore carried the potential for becoming a witch. *I should get her a wand when she's a second level witch.*

A witch of the first level can usually cast spells for luck, love, money or anything she desires but those spells required ingredients, candles, a sacred circle, an athame and many other things. They're quite a hassle and tough work. A witch of the second level can rhyme spells using a wand as a conduit for her powers and her craft is somewhat more effective. At the third level however, a witch can pretty much do anything with her wand, depending on how powerful the wand is of course. There hasn't been any witch reaching the fourth level for centuries, and he had no idea what they'd be capable of once the third level is breeched. He could only imagine that a witch at the seventh and final level of her craft would be pretty much unstoppable. She would be the kin of the Gods.

Bader was sort of happy. His plan for the girls would ensure that he would remain an island. He could use some companionship at times, and he could find that in these girls and Reed. Life was good – or, would be – after Jonathan's death. That same night, they ordered sushi for dinner. They didn't eat in the fancy dining room, but the girls were more comfortable dining in the familiar kitchen. The four of them were as close, in his mind, as he'd ever been to anyone in years.

"You can't face Mr. Jonathan alone," exclaimed Annabelle, who sat next to Darla at the kitchen table.

"I will."

"We have to find him first and then we'll all face him together," Darla added.

"Listen, kids…"

"I'm not a kid," Darla complained. "Am I a kid, Marcus?"

Annabelle smiled. *She feels safe here, and she should.* Annabelle was sixteen, though she looked younger. She was the same age Aurora was when everything fell apart.

"I'm staying out of this…" said Reed just as his cellphone rang. "It's Sera… be right back." Reed went out of the kitchen. "Hello Baby boo". His sing-song version of baby boo echoed back to them and Darla covered her smile with her hand.

"I won't let you fight my battles for me. You killed one of his men but he has five more and …"

Darla suddenly stopped speaking, coughed once, gasped and fell to the floor taking the chair down with her. Bader and Annabelle rushed to her side and found that she was shaking uncontrollably, her eyes wide open. They were white.

The Jade Necklace

Chapter Eleven: Eid el Barbara

"What do you mean you don't want to go to the Barbara party?" Widad asked. She looked down at Clara who had just taken her bed hostage. It was the second of December and winter had come, as *Game of Thrones* fans would say. Widad's bed was small and cozy and she loved to burry herself under its covers. Ever since Erick and Saint Grace-Marie Bou Mansour had made up, Clara had been slightly down. She couldn't say anything, she couldn't speak up nor express herself. And what would she say anyway: "I'm depressed because the man that I love doesn't want me; or I have an unrequited love that needs to be snuffed out of my soul because it is becoming the epitome of unhealthy?"

What was she supposed to tell Andrew or Widad? There was nothing she could do but hold her tongue and hope for the best.

"Well, I really don't feel like mingling with anyone from uni! I thought maybe we could all go up to my place in *Jnoub* and spend the weekend," Clara replied, hiding under the covers.

"I dunno... I really feel like going to the party."

"Let's just go to Jnoub... Besides, since when do you like parties?"

"Well it's a costume party, I was going to go as, well, anything with a big mask on. Also, Fatima and I were supposed to set up the Christmas tree this weekend."

"The tree can wait. I really need to get away from here for a couple of days. It could be good for us. We can relax, watch DVDs all day and maybe have a drink or two."

"Fine, fine, we'll go. But Andy has to come with us." Widad said with a deep sigh.

"Deal!" shrieked Clara as she grabbed Widad's hand and pulled. She fell on top of her with a thud and the girls laughed hard to the point where Clara began to cough. Clara knew that Widad had feelings for Andrew. She wanted, more than once, to burst her bubble but wouldn't dare. She was certain Andrew was gay and felt obliged to warn her best friend but she didn't want to be responsible for starting a rumor concerning the boy's sexuality and losing him as a friend forever.

"Guys! I'm trying to watch Breaking Dawn Part 1! Please be quiet!" Fatima yelled from the living room.

"Hasn't she seen it like... a thousand gazillion times?" Clara laughed. "When does she study?"

As Widad gossiped about her roommate's study habits, Clara's mind drifted towards the vision she had during her out-of-body experience. She couldn't get the monstrous creatures out of her head. She hadn't managed to astral project since that day. She was too afraid. She thought her powers might open a door she may not be able to close. That door might lead her to the man in black and her family but she wasn't strong enough to face all the things she had seen with her astral eyes. The man in black called her an abomination, but she had yet to learn what she was.

The Jade Necklace

****

The third of December was a good day for all of them. It was the eve of Eid Barbara and it brought back so many memories. Clara remembered when she used to dress up like a princess and go from house to house singing *"Hechle Berbara ma'a Banat el hara, refta men idayha w dehkit inayha"*. It was the Lebanese chant for Saint Barbara, a young pagan noble girl who became a Christian. She fled her father's kingdom in disguise and ever since, every Saint Barbara's eve, children dress up in costumes and go from house to house singing her song. Saint Barbara was eventually beheaded by her own father. *Some parents die protecting their little girls while others kill them.*

The friends had gathered at Erick's place before the big trip to the South. Andrew was setting up the Christmas tree. Clara and Widad were playing cards. Erick was in the bedroom, packing his clothes.

"Would you mind helping me out a little?" Erick called from Andrew's bedroom. Clara giggled. *Erick would make a perfect housewife.* He was packing his things, sure, but he was also packing Andrew's things because Lady Andy would never move her butt. Erick did the house chores, cooked, shopped and did everything around the house. The only thing Andrew ever did was put up the Christmas tree. However, in January, Erick was the one who was forced to pack it up again.

"Well, as I'm the only one here who believes in the Christmas spirit, I'm guessing I should be handling the tree," Andrew answered from the living room. "So did you invite Gracie to tag along?"

"Yeah, I did." Erick yelled from the bedroom.

"I'm kind of upset, you know, because we won't get to dress up and go to the party." Andrew put in.

"Clara has costumes in *Jnoub*," Widad said.

Erick walked into the living room with two large bags straddled around his shoulders.

"I love Saint Barbara's. It's even better than Halloween. We get money instead of candy… or at least we used to when we were kids… Hey do you remember that time I dressed up like a gypsy to school?" Andrew asked smiling. *And some still believe he's straight.*

Widad stared at Andy with gooey-love puppy-eyes. *He's in the closet, wake up girl.*

"Yeah and everyone made fun of you," Erick laughed.

"And you had to beat them up," Andrew added shyly. *Does Andy like Erick? Impossible!*

"Yeah, I kind of enjoyed it," Erick said as he sat next to Clara.

"I'm done with the tree," Andrew said. "Let's go and get the girls."

The tree was a beautiful artificial *sapin,* as is referred to in Lebanon. Its green was beautifully sprayed in white that symbolized Christmas snow and was decorated with red ornaments. However, the representation of Baby Jesus and the Saint Family dominated half of the living room space. It had streams of water, mountains, fields, many animals roaming the country side and a large stable where huge figurines resided.

"Who?" Clara asked. "Girls?"

"Gracie and Carmen," Andrew answered.

"What? Who invited Carmen?" Clara shouted. Then, looking around at the blank faces, added: "It's Gracie, isn't it? Ukh...*Fine.*".

***

When they reached Gracie's house, they discovered that Ryan, who was Carmen's brother, was also coming with them. He was smoking a cigarette in his car, windows rolled up. The fog almost masked his brown shoulder length hair and, for a second, Clara almost didn't recognize him. Clara hated Ryan, who also always teased Andy. But she couldn't tell him that he was not welcome now! He'd already been somehow invited and it would've been rude to revoke the invitation.

It was a long way to Clara's house in *Jnoub* and the traffic was hell. When they finally reached their destination, however, the long and tiring journey no longer mattered. They unpacked and divided the rooms as follows: Widad with Clara, Erick with Grace, Ryan with Andrew, and Carmen on her own. Andrew obviously objected to the sleeping arrangement and Clara knew that he was probably going to end up sleeping on the sofa to avoid any time with Ryan.

"So what are we going to do for fun?" Ryan asked as he headed to his room.

"Well, I promised Andrew we'd put on costumes," Erick said.

The Jade Necklace

About an hour later, Clara found herself belly dancing in front of everyone dressed like an Arabian princess.

Afterwards, Erick and Andrew played their childhood song, a "funny" song they had co-written. Erick was dressed like a sexy cowboy. Andrew's costume, on the other hand, confused everyone. He looked like the love child of a butterfly and a used condom.

"I am riding my daughter's bike,

It's too small I'll break the bike" sang Erick.

"I put something on my mouth

So it won't freeze from the cold

You bitch you hoe!" sang Andrew.

However as Andrew said the last line, he accidentally pushed Erick who fell to the ground. Erick was laughing when they all ran to help him out.

****

It was windy and cold. The roads were empty save for the, all too rare, fading streetlights. Gracie hid inside of Erick's jacket wrapped in his arms as they walked down the path flanked, on both sides, by trees. They had changed into their regular clothes. Trailing behind them were Andrew and Clara who both shivered inside their coats. Widad had not joined for the midnight walks, and instead had called it a night early and went to bed. Carmen and Ryan had decided to go check out if there were any nearby restaurants still open.

"I think we should just head back," Clara said, her voice shaking. She rubbed her hands together. "It *is* cold." Andy's lips attempted to smile but shivered into a strange showing of his tiny white teeth clacking against each other.

She watched Mary walk in Erick's embrace. She was warm in his arms. She didn't deserve his love, Clara thought, she didn't deserve to feel him melt in her mouth every time they kissed. Gracie did not deserve that man. She had done nothing to earn his love, and yet she had it. Perhaps that was the key to everlasting love: to be with someone you don't care about, someone you're not willing to make sacrifices for. Then your heart would never be broken and the person would be Yours forever. But what good is that? What good is it to have the love of someone you can't love back? How can that ever turn into true happiness?

"But this is fun," Andrew, who had turned purple from the cold, argued.

"Andy, your ideas of fun are always weird," Clara pointed out. "Look at you. What's fun about freezing?"

The street lights died and all was suddenly quiet. Too quiet, Clara thought.

"Oh, my fuck," Grace cried. "I can't see anything."

"Does anyone have a flash light?" Erick asked but no one said anything. "Let's just head back guys."

But something howled. And whatever it was, it was near.

"What's that?" Gracie whispered into her boyfriend's ear.

"I don't know. Let's move," Erick ordered.

They all turned to see a large black dog with sharp teeth staring at them. Clara was not familiar with dog breeds but she was certain that that was definitely one of the largest and most dangerous breeds to roam the planet.

"Nobody move. And don't show fear," Erick whispered as Grace-Marie clung harder to him.

Andrew was shaking and tears froze on his cheeks. The dog jumped, separating the gang. Gracie tripped as she moved to the side while Clara and Andrew had jumped to the other side. Andrew looked at the dog's drooling muzzle and instantly bounced into the darkness. The rabid dog turned to Erick, barking at him. Erick tried to help Gracie up while Clara still stood frozen.

"Take Gracie home," he shouted to Clara. Then he turned to face the dog which had almost reached him.

"Run home, Gracie. Now!" Clara yelled. She wasn't going to let anything bad happen to Erick, who was now fighting the dog with a stick he had picked off the ground. Gracie ran and the dog did not even notice. It was completely focused on Erick, barking and approaching him, trying to separate him from his herd. She tried to hone her senses, to focus. She wanted to move the dog away from Erick with all of her might and strangely enough... she succeeded. The dog was pulled away and came crashing into a tree. With a whimper, it fled.

They searched for their friend but Andrew was nowhere to be seen. Erick shouted and shouted but met no reply.

"Why didn't you go back with Marie?"

"Because I can protect you."

They continued to run aimlessly in the dark when they heard a young girl scream. They followed the sound until they reached an abandoned house by the end of the street. In front of the house, they saw the dog approaching an unconscious Andrew. *He was probably the screaming girl.* Erick, who was swift and agile, charged at the dog and kicked it in the face. The animal retreated but morphed, suddenly, into a flying beast, a red dragon: large scales, wings, four limbs, and a large muzzle. With one bite, the creature could swallow them whole. It was as large as the abandoned cottage, next to which lay Andrew. The dragon flew towards them, grabbed Erick by the shoulders with its claws and soared. As the creature rose into the night's sky, Clara watched the man she loved being taken away and could do nothing to save him. She tried to use her telekinesis but to no avail.

Erick fought back, struggling to break free from the creature's grasp. But Clara hoped he would realize that if he were freed, he would fall to his death, for they were too high up in the sky. She could barely see them now.

Was that the end? No, she was going to find him. She was going to save him.

The Jade Necklace

Chapter Twelve: Origin

Am I truly innocent?

Childhood, a time of magic: Santa and the fairies could make all the world's troubles go away. I did believe in Santa and every year, since I was eight, I wished for friends. I wished with all my heart that he could help me change schools and start over. What I had been going through was no walk in the park for an eight year old.

Every day, a new tragedy awaited me. I would wake up in the morning and go to class, worried about what the teacher would think when she saw me sitting at my desk alone. All classroom tables were in duplets, yet no one desired to sit next to me. Whenever the teacher asked me to walk to the board, I could hear the whispers: "Be careful, Jane, hope you don't trip." My name is Jonathan, not Jane!

I would pray so hard that the teacher wouldn't hear them so that I wouldn't be embarrassed. The recreation hour was no different. I would spend it eating a sandwich all by myself, except for the brief visits by certain boys who taunted me to impress their friends

It shouldn't be hard to imagine how an eleven-year-old would feel when a boy his age would walk up to him and humiliate him in front of everybody.

"Hey there, Jane. Nice legs!" a guy would shout from afar and my heart would stop. I would cry every time. I tried to ignore him, hoping he would stay away. Always mean boys, always different situations, my true tormentor was a combination of expectations, society, and misogyny.

My tactics to try and "go away" inside my head, as they made fun of me, never worked. A boy once walked towards me with a smug smile on his face and grabbed my hand.

"Will you be my wife?" he asked politely as I tried to free my hand.

"My dick is getting pretty cold and I need to warm it up," the twelve year old said to me. The kids around us laughed. But his sister, who was also there, did not like him bullying me. She had been bullied herself by others because she was overweight.

"Come on, bend over Jane," he said as he forced me to turn, bent me down and rubbed himself against my body from behind. The other kids continued to laugh, but louder now.

I struggled to let go of his hold. Once I did, he shoved me against the wall.

"What? Was I too big for you?" He asked pinning me against the wall.

It was then that his sister rushed back, accompanied by the principal. That was the last day I was bullied by him. He was kicked out of school.

At the end of school days, I would end up on a school bus, in a lonely seat. However, the cool kids who would be sitting behind me would keep throwing things my way while calling me a faggot. At night, I would cry in bed and pray to Baby Jesus. I couldn't tell my parents I wanted to switch schools. I didn't want them to know how cowardly I was. I didn't want to disappoint them.

I truly didn't understand why everyone hated me. What had I done to deserve such treatment? I was good to everyone, always said grace, did as I was told at home, lent my things to classmates, helped them in their homework, yet they humiliated me in return. What was wrong with me?

When I was twelve, I woke up in the middle of the night dreaming of myself in the embrace of a man I had seen on television: Han Solo. I tried to rationalize it at first, thinking that perhaps in my fantasy I was him or wanted to be him. But the same dream haunted me every night for a week until I finally realized what was wrong with me.

One day, I sat next to my mother who was watching television. I couldn't help but notice that two men were talking about how they wanted to be together just like a man would want to be with a woman. I felt relief; there must have been others out there like me. It mustn't have been so wrong for me to want what I want; otherwise it wouldn't be shown on television. I was thrilled and I was smiling when my mother changed the channel and ordered me to go to my room.

"Why? What did I do?" I asked.

"You shouldn't watch things like this," she replied.

"Why?" I asked.

"You're not old enough to understand," she said.

"Try me," I replied, knowing that the recurring dreams meant that I was old enough.

"Honey, sometimes people do bad things. Some people are perverts, faggots, just like these two men. But God doesn't want us to behave that way or else he wouldn't have created a man and a woman. He created Adam and Eve not Adam and Steve!" She explained.

I was shattered; my own mother would hate me if she knew that I was on the path of evil. So I prayed to God! I prayed every night ever since! I did not want to burn in hell for something I didn't choose, something that had chosen me. I hoped He would change me because He was almighty and only He had that kind of power.

God did not answer. I concluded that because I was officially evil, God had abandoned me. If I were to live, I would be a great disappointment to my parents. They will never forgive me and never love me. I felt that my classmates were right all along because, unlike adults, innocent children could see me for who I really was.

Living was suffering. With every breath, I could feel the tears ready to burst out of my eyes. Every night I wished that God would take me in my sleep. If I was meant to choose between suffering here and suffering in hell, I'd gladly choose hell because it would mean that I would not live with the constant risk of causing pain to the ones I love.

That night I found pills in my mom's bedroom.

I grabbed the bottle, tried to read what it said but couldn't understand it. It really didn't matter what the pills were for. All I knew was that I had seen it many times on TV. Whenever someone wanted to die, they would simply swallow a bunch of pills and end their lives. So I decided to take the pills right before I go to bed. I would be dead by morning.

That night, I took the pills in the bathroom one after another. Something deep inside of me wished for mom to catch me. She would stop me, hold me in her arms and tell me that she loved me the way I am. She would tell me that God loved me, and, if He did not, she would no longer love Him. That did not happen and, moments later, I found myself in bed praying for God to make my final moments free of any physical pain. Then, I went to sleep.

The next day I woke up as if nothing happened and my day went on just like any other day, for the next two years. It was a miracle! The Lord had answered in his own way. He told me that He was not finished with me.

I truly wished the world was different. I truly wished that someone would reawaken my innocence and my faith in love but I was too tired. I was sinking to the bottom of a vast ocean and I simply let myself go.

At the time, I believed I wasn't wrong in being who I was. I knew that if there ever was a God, He would have loved me. But I could no longer bear what other men, who claimed to be better than me just because of their heterosexuality, would see me as. I was and am better than many of them, because, unlike them, I did not judge and did not hate irrationally. Unlike them, I knew how to love and how to forgive their ignorance. Yet, it is *their* world.

I truly believed that Harvey Milk was a valiant man, and that one day we would win against the hatred of the misogynistic male.

However, all ended on the day when I truly found the Lord, my savior, and I realized that my very nature was a test to see how true to His word I would be. The world belonged to the misogynistic male because God wills it. Because God wills it, I had to fight my urges and live according to His plan.

***

"He is safe!" I hear a sound coming from the far end of the room. My eyes slowly open but find the light is too blinding although her darkness was very apparent. Isabelle rushes to my side instantly.

"Took you long enough."

"I..." My visions are taking a toll on me. I must have been gone for hours. I look at the clock and find that I've been gone for six hours! Why did I relive the past, remember it so vividly? The lord is trying to tell me something.

But the past is not the only thing that I have seen. I found her hiding spot. The ginger-head phoenix: Darla!

"I found Darla."

I try to get up but find the effort to be far too great.

"Don't move." Her voice is soothing. For a moment I forget that she is the darkness itself. "You need to get your strength back." The room is still out of focus and I can barely see anything around me. I close my eyes for a while.

"We need... to get to work," I command, still seated in my armchair, eyes closed.

The gargoyle hurt me in my vision and managed to kill every single one of my allies, save Isabelle. A plan must be put in place to kill him and kill this girl. Using all of my strength, I stand and open my eyes. We are still at the Brotherhood of the Dawn's headquarters in one of my favorite rooms; the one used for divination. Isabelle goes to the Gypsy table on which a crystal ball is placed and tarot cards are spread on a purple cloth, under the glow of a red wax candle. She stares deep into her divination tool and her eyes turn utterly white.

"What do you see?"

She smiles wickedly and her eyes revert back to the very blackness of her soul. She turns to me and glides towards me to the rhythm of Latin music. She dances around me in circles.

"I found out whose next," her hands are firmly placed on my shoulders as she whispers in my ear.

"We're going to Lebanon."

Her eyes turn to Ahmad, our Fire man. "You're from there originally, aren't you?"

"Iraq," the Arab snarls at her.

"Watch your tone," she replies with absolute poise. I hadn't noticed but the rest of my team weren't there. They were probably resting in their own quarters. We would all need our strength if we were to take on the gargoyle who saved the red head.

"First, we're taking care of Darla," I command. "Leave us"

Ahmad walks out but Isabelle remains.

"You had a vision," she says, "of the past, of the boy you once were, the poor little boy who belonged to the Brotherhood. You're still that scared little boy, aren't you?"

I grab her by the neck and force her back against the wall.

"He's dead and you better remember it," I snarl. But she laughs. Her demonic laughter echoes through the room.

"Is that why you didn't kill Georges? Is that why you asked Jared to cast a tiny spell and send him away? You should have killed him on the spot!? You still love him."

"Get ready," I say. "You do as I order… and keep your nose out of my heart."

Perhaps she is right. But I know what I must do. I have to save the world even if it means sacrificing the one I love. There are only a few phoenixes left in the world and Georges will try to protect them. He will try to stop me. And if he does, I have to kill him, too. Good thing, he has no idea where Darla is. Killing that gargoyle and his deviled phoenix will be easier as long as my lover does not intervene.

Chapter Thirteen: Lessons

Clara closed her eyes in the middle of the street hoping against hope that she would be able to astral project. She wanted nothing more than to find out where Erick had been taken. She would worry about saving him later.

*****

A dragon carried Erick and he could barely see the world below him. He knew he was going to die in a few moments and he had just one wish – to hold Gracie in his arms one last time and tell her how much he loved her.

The dragon landed on the terrace of a big mansion throwing Erick to the ground. Erick stood up, in pain, and the dragon turned into a man. The man was bald, slightly chubby, hairy and, for some reason, naked. *They're always dressed in movies.*

The mansion seemed to be located on a hill top with no other buildings surrounding it. The marble floor of the terrace was completely vacant of the things a villa like this should have: tables, chairs, a pool... The mansion itself was very grey with very few windows. It was too grand and mysterious to be inhabited by anyone who wasn't an affluent political figure or leader of some sort. "My name is Georges. We covered that didn't we?" Georges spoke calmly as he picked up a pair of jeans and a blue shirt off the floor, putting them on as if he hadn't been in the form of a dragon a few moments ago.

"Who the fuck are you?" Erick asked. Anger was pulsating within his vessels and his blood was boiling. The dragon he was afraid of, now a frail old man, was someone he could easily beat to a pulp.

"I think this is the cheesy part where I say I'll give you all answers," a woman's voice said from behind. It was Professor Jennifer Montgomery. She walked towards them in a black night gown. She had seemed to appear from behind the house, probably from a back door.

Erick was in shock. To begin with, he would have never taken her for someone filthy rich. Secondly, she knew about all this supernatural stuff, and that alone was too much to comprehend. Did she have powers similar to Clara's? Was she after him to get to Clara? No matter, he was a good friend and vowed to keep Clara's secret to himself. Although, those two could possibly have answers about Clara's origins. However, he had to tread carefully around them.

"Why don't we go inside? Georges, will you be a dear and make us some tea? Or would you rather have some coffee?" she asked Erick coldly.

"What do you want from me?" he asked.

"Very well, let's skip the small talk. Every time a mage is born…"

"Mage?"

"Spare me. I know you've already been exposed to the supernatural. Your little friend Clara's taken care of that."

"Clara's not..."

"I've seen it. Next time you interrupt, I will turn you into a toad! Now, whenever a mage is born, their soul is branded with a symbol which bestows upon those who carry it an assortment of abilities... why are we branded or how does this come to happen? Honestly, it is beyond my understanding ..." she explained.

"What are you talking about?" he asked. *And who says "bestows" in this day and age?*

"Don't interrupt..." she insisted.

He frowned.

"So every mage is born to a symbol. There's wind mages, such as myself, who are bestowed with the gifts of mind reading, the sight, empathy, levitation, stealing other's abilities, creation of illusions, taking lives away by amplifying a person's emotions..." she explained.

"You can do all those things?" he asked. *Who talks that way?*

"God no... no one can access all of the abilities that their sign provides. I simply have visions of the future and can sometimes access a person's consciousness by touching their hands. I can also dream walk. But enough about me."

Clara was a mage. He was sure now. She was not wind however. Was she? The man in black who attacked her family was probably a mage hunter or something. And her parents, before they died, must have created some form of illusion to shield her from being found again. He had to convince her to stop looking for answers before she opens a door she cannot close.

"I don't understand what this has to do with me…"

"Everything… Clara's heightened hearing and new found capability of astral projection both fall under wind." *Clara can't astral project…or can she?*

"The second sign would be water. Georges here is water and, generally, they have the ability to heal others, as well as invincibility, shape shifting, invisibility, time freezing, and the creation of illusions… Georges can shape shift and heal others when they are injured," she continued. The man dragon stood still by her side. He did not react, did not move. It was as though he was somewhere else completely ignorant of the lessons she was bestowing. *Bestowing... Now I'm using it.*

"How do you know all this?" he asked.

"Then you have earth... no powers whatsoever except that they can turn into witches and that's another story which I will not go into... and, last but not least, fire. They are capable of telekinesis, teleportation, speed, strength, flight, levitation, and they can blow things up at will among other offensive capabilities." *God, it's like she's reading out of a weird encyclopedia.*

Could Clara belong to two signs: fire and wind? Was that why she was special, and therefore, persecuted as a child?

He breathed in the smell of pine trees that surrounded the house and said: "Again, how do you know all this?"

"It was handed down to me through the generations. I know what you must be thinking, Clara, that you are both wind and fire, but you're not."

"Clara?"

"Oh, she's here right now. The girl was worried sick about you and managed to astral project here. Two birds, one stone: even better for me! I hate repeating myself."

"She what...?"

"Now, focus! A very dark man is after you, Erick. His name is Jonathan and he will stop at nothing to kill you. He is working with a witch..."

"A witch?" Erick said. He wondered why Jonathan would come after him. He was no mage, witch, wind, or whatever these people were. He was Erick Haddad, an average Joe kind of guy.

"Witches are born with their power; they are mages who possess the earth sign but are more than mere humans... However, most of them need magic wands to access the supernatural by casting spells. Although, more advanced witches may do so without even uttering words... Isabelle, Jonathan's helper, is not that powerful of a witch for she still uses her wand to this day. But her wand is one of the most ancient and powerful wands ever created."

"Why are they after me? I don't have any abilities... I thought they'd be after Clara... I thought..."

"Jonathan and Isabelle have taken it upon themselves to eliminate all those who possess the fifth sign. The fifth sign only came to existence recently and is known as: the phoenix. It grants its owner access to every single kind of power that has ever existed..."

Does that make Clara a phoenix? She did access the abilities of two different signs. But, it still didn't explain why Jonathan would be after him and not her; unless, he would go after him to get to her. His head pulsated in pain as he tried to listen, hoping that all this would make sense in the end.

"Many might say that Jonathan is right. That a power like that of a phoenix in the wrong hands could prove dangerous. But, I believe that the phoenixes are important for the future of this world. You are a phoenix too, Erick, and sooner or later he will come for you."

"I don't have any powers... I think you got the wrong guy." He wished for a bench to sit on but the only alternative was the floor and he wasn't going to show how much this revelation shook him.

"My visions have led me straight to you… It is you. Your powers are blocked for some reason but I will help you access them…"

"What about the other phoenixes?" He asked.

"You're the second one I found…. The others are either dead, lost, or being tutored by others like me. I belong to the Brotherhood of the Dawn. My brothers and I had made a pact to protect the phoenixes and teach them how to use their abilities."

"What about Clara?" Erick asked abruptly.

"I'm still talking…Isabelle is a dangerous witch because she destroys a phoenix's soul after she kills him or her. That way, they ensure that their powers are forever lost. I had a recent vision, showing me that Jonathan was coming here, that you were next… I sent Georges to fetch you instantly and knew that Clara would watch. And I was right."

"And you know about Jonathan from your visions?" asked Erick.

"No, from Georges... Jonathan killed many people, friends, and family who gave up their lives trying to protect the phoenixes.

"Back in London, Jonathan invaded our headquarters," Georges finally spoke. The older man's eyes had a tint of sorrow and his voice, though poised, was full of bitterness. Or was it gloom?

"That place was supposedly the safest haven for mages from all around the world. He killed every phoenix there except two: Jacob and Darla. Jacob is here with me but we can't seem to find Darla anywhere," Georges added.

"How many? How many are they?" Erick asked.

"We're not sure," Georges answered.

"Five besides Isabelle. But one of them died. You and Clara both need to be trained before the time comes when we have to face them," Professor Montgomery explained.

"Why do you want to help me?" Erick asked.

"Because I believe that phoenixes have a role to play in this world... I believe they are the key to a better future… I need to help shape a better future, Erick, and you're going to be a part of that… but you must speak of this to no one…As for Clara, she and I will have a little chat tomorrow when she comes to visit me after class."

"But isn't she a phoenix, too?"

"No!"

"What is she then?"

"Now go home, and, as of tomorrow, we'll begin with your training," the professor said.

"I have a question. There was a man called Lex who attacked Clara and me in an alley and …" Erick told the story as Jennifer held his hands.

"Close your eyes and imagine this Lex. Remember the alley, yourself, Clara and your attacker; remember what happened," she said. He had barely done what she asked him to do when she gasped.

"Well, you were in great danger," she said as Erick opened his eyes. "Luckily, he doesn't know what you are, but he does know Clara is special. He thinks she's

Fire, but had he intended to attack her again he would've found out she wasn't," she explained.

"What is he?" asked Erick.

"A Makintar: they are immortal creatures that feed off souls to remain eternal. They do so by killing their victims then aspirating their spirit as it leaves the body. They are better nourished by mages than humans but usually avoid powerful ones."

"So he's not coming back?" wondered Erick. *I'm getting used to her dictionary talk.*

"I think after what happened, he'd want to stay away… he's not going to risk his life for a good meal."

"You mentioned a J… Jacob?"

"Jacob is asleep in his room," replied Montgomery. "I think you should head home and do the same…"

***

It was then that Clara found herself thrown back into her body. She was on the couch in her house in Jnoub, Andrew and Widad by her side.

"Thank God you're okay!" Widad exclaimed as Clara opened her eyes.

I am okay but I have no idea what I am.

The Jade Necklace

Chapter Fourteen: The Vision

She looked extremely peaceful. Her face was pale but her breathing was steady and he knew she would be fine. She had a vision the day before and hadn't awoken since. He had no idea what danger she could have foreseen but remained by her side. He passed his rough hand through her silky auburn hair and grinned. What he felt for her was not love. He had only loved once. However, she mattered to him. The likelihood of bonding with another living being as strange and unwanted as himself, was minimal if not impossible. She meant a lot to him simply because she had a good heart. She did not see him as a monster even though that's what he was. He wasn't planning on making babies with her or getting married and settling down, but her friendship and company was much appreciated.

Her eyes slowly opened and the first thing she saw was his smile. He sat on the bed next to her and she tried to sit up straight but couldn't. She appeared to be too tired.

"Hush... It's okay," he said.

"What happened?" She asked weakly.

"You've been unconscious for a day."

She sat up and pushed him away. Her feet touched the ground and she got out of bed. She was scared, he could tell. He stood by her and tried to hold her, to keep her calm. But she pushed him into the dresser.

"He's coming for us... He's... I saw him..." She crumbled onto the ground crying. He hurried to her side and held her. He didn't mean to nor want to; displays of emotions were the things he hated most in the world. But something about that girl in pain drove him to defy his very nature. He held her as she sobbed on his chest. His heart beat faster and his hands shivered as his fingers buried themselves in her soft long hair.

"I'll keep you safe. We're leaving tonight."

He held her face in the palms of his hands and she looked at him through her tearful eyes. He knew she didn't believe him.

"I saw... I..."

"What did you see?"

She put her hand on his forehead and he saw her vision. She had seen Jonathan, his witch and their four warriors break into Reed's home. The witch had turned Reed into a worm then squashed him with her black spiked heels. Bader had managed to take out the four men just before the witch had cursed him into stone, even though it was impossible in his case. In a fit of rage, Darla snapped the witch's wand like a twig then snapped her neck. But, meanwhile, Jonathan was able to destroy the Bader statue. Jonathan and Darla kept fighting until Annabelle's heart was accidentally met by a butcher knife that was meant for her sister. Darla crumbled to her knees beside her dying sister and, as Annabelle released her last breath, Jonathan stabbed Darla in the back. In a fit of rage, she telekinetically snapped Jonathan's neck right before she succumbed to her injuries.

When he came back to consciousness, he was breathless and on the floor. He had only been gone for a minute but had seen enough.

"I won't ... let anything ...happen to you, I promise." He said in between gasps.

"He knows where we are. We need to leave now."

"Get dressed. I'll get Annabelle."

"No. We leave her and Reed here. We're the only ones who can go...."

"Ok... I'll ask Reed to watch over her."

Bader stepped out of the room and ran down the stairs to call Reed.

Reed came out of the kitchen with an apron on. He was covered in flour. Bader, seeing this, gave him the what-the-fuck-are-you-doing look.

"Oh this... well, Annie and I are making cake and..."

"Listen, Reed. Darla and I are taking off for a while, so take care of the little girl. I have no time to explain."

Bader started up the stairs again but Reed made his way towards him and tagged along the rest of the way up. They made their way to the room and found it empty. Darla was gone and the window was open. She had snuck out. She didn't want to put him or her sister in any danger. She wanted to play the lone hero. He should just let her get herself killed as a punishment, he thought.

"I'll check downstairs."

Reed hurried out as Bader looked out the window trying to spot her. It was night and he could morph into the beast that he was and go after her. With his heightened senses he could smell her from anywhere. Her scent was rooted deep within his memories. It was a part of him now. She tugged at his heart with the sheer force of a hurricane and, even though he would never admit it, she was embedded in his very soul. He had no idea when that happened, when he had learned to care about another being again. He couldn't help but wonder if it was some kind of spell, but then it came to him: he cared for her from the moment he chose not to avenge her at the Brotherhood's head quarter. He cared for her when he offered her sanctuary. *I cared for her when we made l… care near the Seine.* He had to find her again. He wasn't going to tell her of what lies in the darkest pits of his charcoal heart, but he was going to keep her safe. She was the first "friend" he'd ever made in centuries and he needed her to remain a part of his life for a long time.

It was then that he heard something breaking downstairs and Reed calling for help.

Chapter Fifteen:
Bader's Phoenix

She was gone. So why would her would-be killers show up at Reed's?

Bader made his way downstairs in seconds to save his friend. He was not entirely surprised to see Reed lying on the floor, blood dripping from his nose. A tall bald man whose belly reached his knees and the witch stood across the room. *Jonathan!*

The man was extremely tall but did not appear to have any particular strength. He had black hair, blue eyes, and a horrendous nose. He was in bad shape: skinny arms and legs around a dangling belly. However, ever since his last encounter with these freaks, Bader knew that he shouldn't judge a person's fighting abilities based on appearance.

"Your friend is not dead, Robin," Jonathan spoke.

Bader froze. "What did you call me?"

"We just want the girl. We mean you no harm," he reaffirmed. Jonathan wasn't lying. Bader was certain that he would leave them alone if they handed Darla over. But, if the man was an all-powerful seer then why would he look for her at Reed's, unless he was relying on her abilities to defeat her? He could have been trying to lure her back, to attack her sister and friends, thus provoking a vision that would send her running back into a trap.

"Just like you meant all of those people no harm?"

"They tried to fight us. It was self-defense... We didn't kill all of them... Those that surrendered were allowed to leave and they were many. Give us the girl and we'll leave you two alone. We don't want to harm Annabelle, nor you, nor Reed."

"Where are the rest of your friends?" Bader tried to examine the room to see if he could find any evidence of a third or fourth camouflaged attacker. His hearing tried to sense anyone else in the house... Those two were alone.

The witch's eyes moved past Bader and locked on a spot behind him. She smiled and giggled wickedly like a psychotic bitch. Bader turned around and saw that Darla was behind him. She had come back! *No!*

"If you want me, come and get me."

"There's our girl," Jonathan said as he stepped in front of a grandfather clock that's been in Reed's family for generations.

Bader turned around as Darla looked into his eyes and he understood that his fear was justified. Jonathan attacked them in order to lure her back in and he had succeeded. She came back to save him and that made it his duty to protect her. Bader ran towards the witch meaning to snap her neck when the belly man sent a lightning bolt at him, incapacitating him. As Bader lay breathless on the floor, Darla leaped at Jonathan while managing to avoid all of his lightning bolts. She jumped in the air and kicked him right across the face and sent him crashing into the grandfather clock.

Jonathan on the ground, Darla grabbed the witch by her hair and banged her head against the wall and then, still pulling at her hair, she squeezed her hand so hard that the witch had to drop her wand. It was then that Annabelle came in through the door to the kitchen. *Run, kid, run.*

Bader managed to get back on his feet. Jonathan raced at him. However, this time Bader was prepared. He had turned into a gargoyle. He wrapped his tail around the man's legs and beat his wings to rise up a bit, then threw the man out of the nearest window.

"Jonathan!" The witch cried stepping on Darla's leg. *We're on the ground floor cunt!*

"Your turn." The gargoyle headed towards her with a deadly grin. She scratched Darla's hand and made for her wand. Skin and blood under her nails, she almost reached it but Annabelle beat her to it. Yet, the moment Annabelle tried to grab the ancient wand, she was electrocuted and was sent flying. The girl bumped her head on the stairs and passed out. *Is she alive?*

By that time, Jonathan had climbed back in to where they were. With one swift lightning bolt, the tables were turned. The bolt hit Bader's abdomen and injured him badly. Blood was gushing out of him. Bader fell to the floor, his surroundings dimming. But he could still witness, though everything was blurry, the events that took place.

Darla herself threw a lightning bolt at Jonathan hitting his shoulder. This gave the witch enough time to pick up her wand.

"From now till my work is done

Frozen shall be the foe I see

You cannot move until I've won

And there will be no remedy." The witch chanted, and both Darla and Bader found themselves paused, like statues, in the middle of the action, unable to move.

"Spirits of the wind, spirits of the earth, spirits of the waters, and spirits of the flames,

I call upon thee to form my circle."

Reed was back to semi-consciousness by then, stood up, and tried to grab the witch. But, Jonathan telekinetically threw him against the wall. Reed fell to the ground, a few steps under Annabelle, bleeding from his scalp. He did not move after that.

The witch's eyes were blood red. She and Darla were face to face in a hurricane, a sphere made of the four elements: water behind the witch, fire behind the victim, wind on the witch's left, and earth on the witch's right. It was very much like the sphere she was trying to create at the Brotherhood's headquarters, only on a smaller scale.

Bader struggled to move but could not. He kept on looking at Reed hoping that he would wake up in time and manage to break the witch's wand. He struggled to move but he was completely paralyzed. His muscles strained and he felt a thousand blades tear at them whenever he'd try to use them.

"Her soul is yours to devour for heaven rejects such a blasphemous child,

Too wicked for hell, I feed her to the fire..."

The witch chanted as the flames embraced Darla's body. Her screams pierced his ears. *Come on, Reed. Wake up!*

"Too harmful to the earth its mother, that it demands her death! I feed you her essence. O, great sands of time."

The chant went on. Now, floating rocks and pebbles appeared and stoned the scorching Darla.

Bader was hopeless. The hold on him was greater than any he'd ever felt. Nothing could break him free, nothing could save his phoenix.

"Not even Angels may save this evil. No purity lies inside this carcass. O, howling winds of emptiness, I give to you the sacrifice you crave."

She chanted again as the wind blew causing the fire to intensify. Darla screamed out in pain, which made Bader keener to save her. To scream means to be alive and there was still a chance. Her screams may be able to compel him to break free of the witch's spell. If pain forced her to scream then perhaps the fear of losing her could force him to call out to Reed. He tried to open his mouth, to speak up, to shout, but could not. He hoped that the pain that she was going through would help him move. Perhaps if he started moving something as simple as his toes or fingers. He tried to wiggle his finger, to bat his eyelids, to do anything! But he was as still as a rock, and his heart beating incessantly was the only part of him that was not frozen.

Reed was starting to wake up, to move. When he raised his head and looked at Darla and the witch, Bader had some hope again.

"Extinguish her life oh great water, source of life! O, great waters of existence, extinguish what you once created, destroy the essence of this atrocity! I beseech thee!"

The witch's nose started bleeding, and the wall of water crashed onto her and Darla. They seemed to be drowning inside a sphere of water that engulfed the entire room. Reed managed to stand up and run at the wall of water.

Save her!

Reed crashed into the wall of water and was swallowed within the sphere, too. He was trapped within the wall of water, separated from the outside world. He flapped about like a fish caught in a hunter's net. Despair seeped out of Reed's eyes, and Bader knew that his friend could be lost at any moment. He kept trying to force himself to move, to crash into the witch and bite her head off but it was too late and Reed had stopped wiggling. A few moments later, the high walls of water which had consumed his companions gave into gravity and flooded the entire living room.

Jonathan bled all over the mansion's carpet as he made his way towards his servant witch. Bader, water reaching above his ankles, tried to move. He needed to save her. He had to. Furious now, he needed to kill. His heart was made of darkness and it knew how to hate, how to kill, how to feed.

"Is it done?" Jonathan asked breathlessly.

"Yes..."

They both walked out. Bader regained motion soon, but fell to the floor because of the deadly wound. Darla was charred and did not move. Reed lay motionless on the floor next to her. And Annabelle was unconscious or dead and bleeding.

Bader forced himself to stand up and ran in the direction the intruders had gone. When he caught up with them, he grabbed Jonathan with his paws as he had done the vampire the other night and took off into the sky. He was losing blood and consciousness but kept on flying until he reached a river he knew well. Blood dripping from his wound had covered Jonathan's face and eyes. He knew Jonathan could not use any powers against him because he had none. Darla wasn't around for him to access her powers and his mindless zombies weren't anywhere close. He was losing altitude and his surroundings were turning into a haze. He suddenly felt forced to let go of Jonathan. To drown in a river was too merciful a death but better than no death at all. He did not hear a splash but couldn't dwell on it any further for he was losing his strength. He was losing consciousness, and in his weakened state, morphed back into a man. A gargoyle flies, yes, but a man cannot. He fell and fell and fell, gaining momentum until he splashed into the river. He was unable to swim, to resurface. The current was too strong and knew that this could very well be the end of him. He swallowed water.

Dawn broke and the new-born rays of sun hovered above the river. Bader yearned to live another day, if only to avenge the ones he cared for. Darla, Reed, Sera, their kids and Annabelle were his family, the only family he could ever have. He was going to avenge every bit of harm brought upon him and his!

But he swallowed more water as the current took him.

No one takes what is mine and lives.

But the current was too strong. No man was strong enough to swim against it...

The Jade Necklace

Chapter Sixteen: Some Training Required

Erick and Clara were in the car, under her dorm building. He told her everything. He apparently found it hard to believe that Clara was really there when Montgomery told the story. And he thought that it wasn't true: "She's crazy! I'm not a phoenix and this "Jonathan" isn't after me," he told her.

Clara had to tell him that she truly did have the ability to astral project and they played the "how many numbers am I holding behind my back" game to prove it. However, as usual, Clara couldn't truly control her powers. She came to the sad realization that she could only access her abilities when she was scared or angry.

The hard part was hiding the truth from their friends. On the night of Saint Barbara, Ryan was the one who found her and Andrew out in the street. He took them back home where they were cared for, and she slowly regained consciousness. However, Ryan had gone back out to search for Erick.

The story they decided to tell was that a rabid dog had attacked them and they were all lucky to escape without getting bitten. When she woke up, Clara was not worried about Erick but had to feign her emotions until he returned home. He explained that he got lost and everything was swept under the rug. It was the first time they lied to Andrew and Widad. The first of many times, she believed.

"I'm really glad I'm not alone in this anymore but if I am not a phoenix, then what happened to me in Geneva? Why do I have powers?"

"I think you're the real phoenix …" Erick said.

"Well, I think you've got what it takes to be one. I suppose I could have that little chat with Montgomery. It just makes me feel… It's bad enough not knowing where I come from and why all those people were after me! And now someone wants you dead," she continued.

"We've got each other's backs don't we? I'm a phoenix, remember? I'll protect you."

"Well, I'm the one with the active powers for now so I'll be protecting you from that Jonathan guy." she explained, smiling with pride.

"I love you," he said, seemingly drowning in her eyes. Her heart skipped a beat and time seemed to stand still for hours, even days. She smiled at him and leaned forward, wetting her lips, ready for a true love's kiss. "You're one of my best friends. We'll protect each other," he said as disappointment ravished her face.

"Me too," she affirmed, and then added: "I need a place to sleep... they won't let me in tonight, I'm sure."

Clara hated her dorm's rules. No one was allowed to stay out past midnight, which is why she had to spend countless nights sleeping over at other people's place.

"Sure." He drove off.

****

They reached the mansion early in the morning. They found that the door was open. They stepped in hesitantly. Clara was awed by the magnificence of the Louis XIV-style entrance. She had no idea how Professor Montgomery had made her fortune and wasn't about to start asking. As they reached the marble stairs leading upstairs, a fire ball was hurled in their direction. Clara telekinetically diverted it out the window. A few meters away from them, a cocky young man stood cracking up with laughter. She was startled and scared. That's how she accessed her active powers. Fear was the trigger.

"I'm sorry," the young man said as he continued to laugh. He couldn't have been older than twenty: dirty blonde spiky hair and a toned body, silly Chinese tattoo on his right shoulder, a sleeveless tight shirt. She could have possibly found him hot if she didn't feel like punching the smile off his face.

Professor Montgomery elegantly glided downstairs in a white turtle neck suit that covered every inch of her skin.

"Most impressive," she said.

"Who is that?" Erick asked, pointing at the laughing boy.

"That's Jacob. He's a phoenix ... Georges is training him," she explained. "Something big is coming. The great concern right now is that there are 12 phoenixes left in the whole world and only 10 of them are adults or adolescents. One of them lives in Beijing and doesn't even know of her powers. I have contacted a friend of mine and asked him keep an eye on her. The others are already in training by devoted members of the Brotherhood except for the two children. They are too young to train and too young to be detected by Jonathan at the moment"

"That's good right?" Clara asked.

"You and I should have a talk, Clara."

She walked into another room and Clara assumed that she was expected to follow, and follow she did.

Professor Montgomery sat on a beautiful Persian couch in the middle of an 'Ancient Persia' themed living room.

"Does every room have a particular theme?" *Everything I think sounds silly when said out loud.*

The Jade Necklace

"You are very powerful, dear." Professor Montgomery started, ignoring her question. "But if you want answers, I'm not the one that can give them all to you," she explained.

Professor Montgomery told Clara that she was an anomaly. Clara was born without a sign: she was not a mage, she was not a human but was part of both worlds somehow. She was the impossible and there was no explanation as to why she had come to exist. The secret, she believed, lied in finding her parents and sister again because their family must have been very special. Professor Montgomery promised to help Clara as much as she could and sent her off to train with Georges.

****

"They're training, relax," Professor Montgomery was watching from her window when Georges reassured her. She had taken one look outside, only to see Clara fly across the terrace and land on Professor Montgomery's Infinity G, one of her many cars, Clara presumed. Georges was downstairs training with Clara, Erick and Jacob, à la boot camp style, while Professor Montgomery watched on from above.

Clara couldn't let the Professor assume that the misogynistic terror of a boy was stronger than her. She leapt to her feet and telekinetically threw Jacob, pinning him against Professor Montgomery's window. The evil hag, who was neither evil nor a hag, smiled. *Strangely she reminds me of Ursula from the Little Mermaid. I can imagine her singing "Poor Unfortunate Souls" and seducing Erick.*

Clara was, for reasons beyond her control, too angry to think straight and that was when her powers came most naturally to her. She had something to prove. She was the only one who could protect Erick and needed him to believe in her.

"Phoenix, my ass... I can wipe the floor with you, anytime," she insisted, when a jolt descended from her neck, down her spine and filled her fingers with a fiery energy. A power surge was released through her fingers and before she knew it, Jacob was being electrocuted by what seemed to be Jedi powers. Beams of electricity escaped her fingers tips and converged on the boy's body.

"Oops. What just happened?" Clara managed to stop. She was in awe and looked apologetically at Professor Montgomery. She floated the boy to the ground and rushed to his side as he coughed incessantly.

"You just accessed a new power," Professor Montgomery said proudly as she opened the window and leaned against the windowsill.

Jacob, still coughing, managed to throw a low level fire ball at Clara, hitting her in the shoulder. Clara lost focus. Jacob stood up and threw many fire balls straight at her. Fireballs floated in midair all around her, finally forming a cage that trapped her.

"Care to give up now?" he asked sarcastically.

"Never," she replied as she let loose the electricity which he managed to avoid by levitating in the air and forcing the bars of her fiery cage to melt together into a sphere that forbade anything from exiting.

"Give it up before you run out of oxygen in there," Jacob insisted.

"Stop it now," Professor Montgomery yelled, "Jacob!"

Clara looked towards the window but did not see her. When the boy complied, she realized that Professor Montgomery had come outside to interfere.

"That ought to teach you not to mess with a phoenix," he said to the breathless Clara. *Where the fuck is Erick?*

****

On their way back, Clara couldn't help but express how much she hated Jacob. He was really hot. *Man!* His body surpassed the wonder that Erick's body had always been. However, the boy had too much arrogance. She couldn't believe that Erick did not come to her aid because Georges forbade him. "Phoenixes don't attack each other," said that silly man. If Erick truly loved her, he wouldn't have listened, he would have beaten Jacob to a pulp. Then again, Erick never loved her and probably never will.

"When you get your powers we need to team up and kick Jacob's ass. Phoenix code of honor my ass!" she concluded. Erick agreed.

The Jade Necklace

Chapter Seventeen: The Three Bitches

Three little bitches, that was the plan.

Shireen was the queen of this little clan.

Three they were when they reached the party,

And Grace-Marie, couldn't help but be naughty.

Shirtless men all around, as if it were a pool party.

Carmen sandwiched between two hunks the girl knew how to get cocky.

Up on a chair, in her bra,

Shireen was eyed by all in awe.

The Jade Necklace

She danced and laughed and winked at him;

But when they kissed, she let go of that whim.

Plenty of men to go around,

Only the best kisser gets to be her hound.

A hottie bid her to sit on his lap, Grace-Marie did not say no.

She got off later because he was full of crap. But not before snapping a photo of her fake beau.

"Hey what's up" said another guy,

staring Gracie straight in the eye.

"I have a boyfriend" she should've said,

 But she buried the idea in the back of her head...

Instead they danced and as she acted coy,

But she did not – surprisingly- kiss that boy.

Three had come but four had left,

And Shireen was not alone in her bed.

Chapter Eighteen: Eric's Flame

She moaned in ecstasy as he devoured her thighs while slowly stroking her clitoris with his middle finger. His hazel eyes met hers and her body shook beneath him like a leaf. His breath was on her neck. Her hands found their way onto his muscular back and she delicately caressed it with the tips of her fingers. Extending her neck for the taking, her right hand forced his head onto it and he ravaged it with his tongue. He kissed and licked her skin until her moaning echoed in the whole apartment. *We're lucky Andrew isn't here.*

His hand closed in on her lips and she bit it. The pleasure was too intense. He looked into her eyes again and smiled. She was sweating, shaking, and happy. He was the reason behind it all. His hand moved down from her lips and cupped her bare breast, his other hand between her legs. She was wet, his fingers were soaking in her pleasure. The mere thought of pushing himself inside of her, made him feel like a man. He was her man, the only man whom she'd allow to do that to her.

His tongue made its way towards her pink nipple and he suckled on it, before making his way down. He engulfed her wetness in his mouth and savored every drop of it. Her moans stimulated his tongue to delve deeper into her. Her smell was enticing: strawberries. *She used a chapstick again, I love her.*

"Fuck me." Gracie groaned before he slowly licked his way back up to her nipple. He cupped her breast and suckled as her toes contracted multiple times and her leg eventually kicked the foot of the bed. His lips then found hers. His stiffness was rubbing against the wetness, a natural lubricant, and he knew that he couldn't wait any longer. He almost pierced her with his member but she closed in her legs around him and stopped.

"Not like this..." She said.

"How do you want it?"

She forced him off of her and got on all fours. The blood had completely abandoned his brain at that point. Her soft pink bubble butt was in his face and he wanted nothing but to nibble on it. He spread her cheeks open and a soft pink hole winked at him. He knew she wouldn't let him enter her from behind but that didn't mean he couldn't pretend.

"Give it to me baby."

He grabbed a condom from the dresser and put it on. He then clutched her by the ass and slowly penetrated her. A tight wetness squeezed him and he could only imagine how much tighter her other hole would have been.

"Harder," she groaned as he began to love her with an ever increasing acceleration.

The harder he gave it, the more she wanted it. He was on fire, fighting the urge to climax before the time was right. He grabbed her by the hair with one hand, straightening her back and kissed his way from his neck to her mouth. Her tongue inside his mouth, wiggled at his inner cheeks and palate simulating a weird numbness. He stroked her clitoris with the other hand till they both reached their peak. Her muscles contracted around him, milking him dry into the condom and he couldn't help but wish to empty his load inside of her.

"I love you baby," she said breathlessly as he pulled out.

He took her in his arms.

******

It was windy and cold. The clouds had curtained the moon and, though there were streetlights, it was darker than usual. Clara thought of Erick and how they could have taken a walk together hand in hand. She was numb to the cold beneath her layers of clothes, and her ears were tucked away beneath her hair and the red hood of her jacket. She couldn't help but wish being numb around Erick as well. She wondered what it was that Erick did not find in her but did in Grace-Marie. Clara loved him with all her heart but he wasn't about to love her back.

Her phone beeped. It was a text from Widad with screenshots of what Shireen had posted on her Instagram about the three bitches' wild night the day before. Gracie was sitting on a guy's lap in a picture and dirty dancing with the bouncer in another.

She smiled yet felt wicked. This was her chance to show Eric who the girl he loved really was. This was her chance to earn his love. But what kind of love is it if she knew it would hurt him? What kind of love would compel her to harm him and shred his heart?

Widad finally called her. "We should tell him!" She shouted. "I'm telling him."

"No! We still have finals this week. Let's wait until the semester ends, and then we tell him," Clara argued.

*****

It was not a crowded night at the library, as finals were coming to an end. Clara and her friends had seated themselves on a small table at the back of the large rectangular library, near stacks of books. As per usual, she was supposed to be accompanied by Erick, Andrew, and Widad but the four were joined by the she-demon who was actually done with her finals and had just come along to annoy them.

"I think everyone is PFSing," Andrew said, while Clara examined the worried expressions on the students' faces.

"What's that?" she asked.

"Pre-finals syndrome." Andrew jokes, and Clara smiled.

"So the nightmare ends tomorrow!" Grace-Marie said, hugging Erick.

"I thought you were done," Clara said.

"Yeah, but I'm here to support my Poo Panda."

But Clara, seeing Erick smile, wasn't going to let them start kissing again.

"Hey Poo Panda, how about some studying?" Clara said.

"My Poo Panda will run for president someday. But first, he has to stop being a *waitress*." Grace-Marie laughed.

"What the fuck?" Erick snorted.

"You're working in a restaurant?" Clara asked. "How come I don't know?"

"I..."

"He's a branch manager," Andrew replied. "Good for him, he's making some money unlike the rest of us."

"I was just teasing you babe don't worry about it. We all know you want to get published one day. You'll be the poor waiter guy who turns into a big success... or not."

No one could tell what was wrong with Grace-Marie. She was very loving at times and at other times very destructive. Clara always thought that it was because Gracie fed off other's insecurities as a way of feeling better about herself, just like Carmen. However, no excuse could justify the bullying of the man she supposedly loved.

The following day was to mark the end of it all; the end of a semester, at least. Clara feared losing her 4.0 GPA and honor list status. Erick, on the other hand, was full of self-confidence and knew that, wherever you threw him, he would land on his feet. That's at least how Clara perceived him. The boy never nagged about studying, never complained about his grades. He was destined for greatness, she thought. He was destined for greatness, if the she-demon would steer clear of his path.

The next day, when their nightmare ended, Andrew and Clara walked out of their exam arguing about the answers. Erick joined them.

"So how did you guys do?" He asked.

"We don't want to talk about it. It's bad luck," Andrew said.

"Well, I'm glad that's over. Let's do something fun," Erick said.

"Don't you mean sleep?" Clara asked.

"No! How about brunch?"

"Okay. But you're driving me to bed straight after. Your bed, of course, I am really not in the mood to see Carmen," Clara complained.

"No comment," replied Erick as they all walked out of the faculty.

"I'm texting Wido. I'll tell her to meet us at Khan El Wared." Andrew suggested.

"Sure, man."

Clara wondered if Erick wanted to text Grace-Marie. However, she was almost sure that he was still upset about the scene she had made the night before. But was he upset enough to not invite her?

The night before, when the five friends had finished studying, they went for a midnight snack when Grace-Marie utterly embarrassed Erick again in front of everyone.

"Baby, you're paying for my sandwich because you still owe me ten dollars from the other night... Oh, unless you're broke again tonight."

Clara could tell that her words cut him deep. Erick had always assumed that a relationship was about sharing. He had shared everything that he had with Grace-Marie and spent a lot of his hard earned cash on making her happy but the girl was never thankful. More so, she humiliated him in front of his close friends and not for the first time. His heart and mind were her domain, however, and there was nothing that anyone could do to change that. Clara was certain that nothing could change how he felt about her.

****

Erick parked the car far away from his apartment building as he couldn't find a parking space. As he, Clara and Andrew strolled towards the boys' building, his phone rang. It was Gracie. He hesitated but then answered. He wondered if she had found out that he was hanging out with the gang without her. He couldn't bear to look at her after how she treated him the other night but answered anyway. He could handle the hurtful words she'd always hurl his way, the insults. He could handle her lack of faith in him. He had gotten used to all that and it only took him a few days to heal before he'd jump back into the relationship. The one thing he could never handle was infidelity and he had seen her pictures at that party with her friends. He had seen them the night before but didn't want to bring it up, hoping that she would first. He would then forgive her for coming clean. But she didn't! Instead, she salted his wound by humiliating him in front of their friends. He wasn't going to take it anymore.

"You went partying this weekend, didn't you, *babe*." Erick said with no hesitation. And a long argument soon followed.

"I can't do this anymore! You're suffocating me!" Gracie screamed, and Clara – thanks to her super-hearing abilities – was surely listening. He knew she listened but didn't care.

"It feels like I'm in some sort of prison when I'm with you!" Gracie yelled. Andrew and Clara were a few paces away from him listening, looking to the ground.

"How do you think I feel?" he yelled. "You always fuck up. Every time I feel safe with you, every time I feel like you really are the girl of my dreams, you do something to mess me up! What the hell is wrong with you?"

"I don't want to do this anymore!" This is too much for me! You're too much!" she retorted.

"This isn't the first time you do this!"

The Jade Necklace

"I love you," she said calmly after pausing for a few seconds. "You're just too good for me." And she hung up.

Erick picked up his pace and went back to his car.

****

He was going to see her, Clara knew that. It wasn't nice of him to leave them on the street but she knew the urgency of the situation. Whenever Gracie would break up with him, Erick would turn into a puppy dog.

"I need to take a nap," Clara said. She rushed to the apartment and went into Erick's room. The room was very neat and equipped with most of the high tech things (that Clara had no comprehension of) you'd find in a tech savvy boy's room. Unlike other boys their age, Erick's room was very neat so Clara had to open his closet in order to reach for one of his T-shirts. She lay on the bed, tugging the shirt closely to her heart hoping against hope that she could astral project and see what was about to happen.

Grace-Marie had just hurt the boy she loved. He was angry at her for lying and taking sexy photos with horny guys and yet, somehow, she still made it seem as though he had hurt her and, therefore, broke up with him. Was Erick really being that old fashioned and too Lebanese in his mentality? She knew she would never do what Gracie did. But it wasn't like Gracie had sex with someone. She was just at a party, drunk and dancing around with guys. These thoughts gave her a headache and she finally found herself watching over Erick.

If he ever finds out I'm using my powers to spy on him...

****

Erick drove recklessly until he reached Gracie's apartment building and honked. She didn't come out, until he rang her on the interphone. He went back to his car to wait until she came out. It took her a few minutes to emerge, eyes all red.

"What the hell is wrong with you?" he yelled stepping out of his car yet again.

"I can't be in this relationship. It's not working out for me!" she said without opening the building's iron-gate.

She spoke to him through the bars as though she feared that he would hurt her.

"People don't break up over quarrels," he headed for the gate and stood there. She wasn't within reaching distance. She really feared him and for the life of him he couldn't understand why.

"My parents are upstairs. Don't make a scene," she insisted.

"Don't tell me what to do."

"I'm going back up. Just go away! I don't want to do this!" she said as she turned back. She was going to leave, to go into the elevator but he couldn't let her. He extended his arm and reached in as far as he could, grabbing her with a tight grip. *She really wasn't within my reach.*

"Why?" he said firmly. She cried out in pain and he let her go.

"Because you're too good for me," she said and struggled to break free of his hold.

"Don't you dare walk away!" He squeezed at her skinny arm. *Yesterday you said you loved me!*

"Let me go right now or I'm calling the police!"

He obliged. She went into the elevator and shut the door behind her. The elevator went from: RC to 1 to 2 to 3 and then it stopped again. She was home.

****

"Gracie broke up with me," he said as he cracked up laughing.

Clara and Erick were lying in his bed while Andrew sat at the edge and observed silently. She held him in her arms under the covers.

"You are too good for her," she insisted.

"How could she do this to me? Every time I think we've gotten really close, she... God, I don't even know her anymore."

"She's always been this way," Clara said.

The window was open and as a cold breeze serenaded her long hair, she couldn't help but smell the trash.

Beirut had been in a trash crisis for some time... they had run out of places to actually throw the garbage. Hence, everything was left out on the streets for the gutter rats. The smell had been avoidable the first few weeks but by that day, any form of air movement would burn anyone's nose with the smell of garbage.

She was in a very confusing state of mind. *Lebanon has a trash crisis and I have an Erick crisis.* Although, she was happy that Gracie was finally out of the picture. She truly believed that even though he might never love her, he deserved better than Grace-Marie. However, she hated to see him suffer, for that made her suffer as well.

"I think you guys should stay away from each other for a while," she explained, a pincer grasp around her nose. She knew that a person could never be friends with someone they're in love with.

"I can't do that. She's our friend," he insisted nasally.

"You're going to be hurting yourself that way. If you still see her, I mean." *What the hell is up with the smell! Ugh!*

"I can take care of myself," he said as she held him tightly.

"I hate it when you're suffering. I just want you to be happy again."

He held her hand. The only person to ever give her goosebumps was him. Why was life that unfair? Why couldn't people just fall for those who were willing to love them back? Why did she have to suffer so?

For the first time ever however, Clara had hope that he would be hers. And then she remembered that this had happened too many times before. She remembered that she'd had that same hope after every break up. But hope was rudimentary to her survival, for the thought of living without the hope of his love was a death sentence.

"I can't believe she pretended to cry…" Clara said aloud.

"I never told you she was crying…"

"Yeah you did, you said she was crying before you got there and…"

She was nervous. Was he onto her now?

"Did you? Clara? I'm going to ask this one time and you're going to answer me," he was dead serious. He was more serious than he'd ever been in his entire life. She knew that he was going to take out all his built up frustration on her.

"Did you?" He didn't finish his question because both realized that Andrew was still with them in the room. Andrew did not dignify the awkward silence with a comment, and simply retreated out of the room, shutting the door gently behind him.

"Clara you had no right to invade my privacy."

"I'm sorry."

"I need to be alone now."

"But…"

"Please."

She slowly got to her feet and walked out of the room, hoping that he would stop her. He uttered no words, and made no gestures. She closed the door behind her and knew that he was going to take out his frustration on her little mistake. She risked losing her best friend due to her powers and, for the first time in her life, she hated being special.

Chapter Nineteen:

Revenge

Rain washed over the monster standing on top of the cathedral. In the dark, he could have easily been mistaken for a statue. But he was very much alive. His red eyes pierced the veil of night for he was hunting. The rain brought forth the smell of the earth, rain initiated a new cycle of life. It would bring him back to the beginning, to his origins: a monster! From up high, he could see the entire city. He hadn't fed off a human in a few weeks and his hunger needed to be quenched. He had taken up the habit of sleeping after sunset in order to keep the beast at bay. It worked for some time. There was a time, long ago, when he had slept every night to avoid the bloodlust, but that was a forgotten past. He was a different man then. No not a man, a boy. Long ago, he didn't lust for blood not even when he'd morph into a gargoyle for he had a pure heart. After darkness took hold of his heart he realized that to go into a deep sleep or to remain calm is most likely to keep his inner beast at bay whenever the night would come and he had done so for over a century. Unfortunately, no man could resist his inner nature. His hunger kept growing and gnawing at his soul. Ever since he bonded with Darla, he attempted to fight off the urge to tear apart a human being for dinner. He had managed to resist his inklings almost every night.

This night was different, however. The hunger was unappeasable and he needed to hunt men. Perched on the tallest tower, he watched the empty streets. Reckless thoughts invaded his mind. Could he have become so deprived of his humanity that he'd be willing to break into people's homes to feed? He couldn't! He wouldn't!

A monster! Darla had called him. A monster, he might have been, but he truly wanted to protect her. It wasn't love, that much was obvious. He had only loved one woman his whole life and was certain that there won't be another whom he would allow into his heart. However, when he met Darla, a part of him, the part that died with Aurora, was rekindled. He could have loved Aurora eternally, had she still been around. As for Darla, they were both kindred. She was the first kindred soul he had met in centuries... and they killed her. He tried to kill her murderer but his witch must have cast a spell to save him from falling into the strong current. Bader almost lost his life in the process for he had fallen into the waters. A gargoyle is immortal but not invincible. But he knew he wasn't going to die. He had a vengeance to seek. In spite of his human form, he was still strong. He tried to swim with the current until he reached the border. He still could not resurface but tried as hard as he could to hold on to an edge, to a root, to anything he could find. He tried as much as was possible but could not. He breathed in the frozen water and it filled his lungs. He was freezing, drowning. He almost gave up. If it weren't for the root that suddenly came upon him, he would have. He pulled as hard as he could, further exacerbating his wound. He pulled harder and harder, fighting the urge to scream. Revenge became his strength and he pulled himself out, lay by the river bank and coughed out the water. He then went into a deep slumber.

Angered and enraged by the memory, he flew into the storm. It was as turbulent as his soul. It rained heavily but that didn't stop him from reaching the alley where a fight had erupted. Two men took to the beating of a third who had been bloodied by the time he had reached them. The beast landed in the midst of the clash causing the offenders to take a step back. He carried both men into the sky by digging his claws through their backs into their very lungs. He was engulfed in darkness. The victim could not see his evil savior.

The gargoyle flew into the gloomy sky, with his hemorrhaging preys that were too breathless to shout or cry for help. He took them to Reed's home where he could make a meal of them in peace.

When he was done feeding, he morphed back into his naked human form, put on his jeans and went down to the living room to find Reed.

"I thought you went to pick up Sera from the airport."

"No." Reed said with a barely audible voice. "Oh right, I should probably put something on." Bader smirked.

"You have something on your..." Reed pointed out Bader's bloody face and the latter wiped off the red with tissue papers.

"I should wash up before I go looking for her."

"Are you sure you want to go there?" the frightened Reed asked.

"Stop being a pussy." Bader walked away. "And you're not going... you need to have a conversation with your wife."

Bader had decided that Annabelle should stay with Reed and Sera in their loving home. He wasn't going to send Darla's sister out there where she could barely fend for herself. He owed Darla that much, he had to keep the girl safe. Jonathan wasn't going to go after Annabelle again but still. The girl had no money and was still a minor. She needed someone to look after her. Reed was perfect for that.

"I don't think it's safe for you to go off on your own..."

Reed was right. The crone, Mama Jinguala was truly strange, even dangerous but he had to seek her out. Mama Jinguala was a seer and she was the only one who could help him find the revenge he sought.

She had first come to him when he was fifteen. He and Princess Aurora had snuck out of the King's castle. They both knew that her father would be too angry with them but they did it anyway. They were in love and wished to be alone. They wanted to swim in the small lake just south of the castle, kiss under a tree, run in the open fields, and possibly make love for the first time.

When they reached the stream he blushed. He was afraid of taking his clothes off in front of her. She was as terrified as he was, he believed. Her face was the red of an apple and her eyes dared not meet his.

"Robin?" she asked in a whisper upon the breeze.

"I do not believe we should go for a swim, Princess."

"I believe we should..."

He walked towards her and his hand gently brushed against her arm. It made her smile shyly. She buried her face into his chest and he knew he would never love this way again. She was a princess and he was merely a commoner. But he loved Aurora since the moment he had laid eyes on her and a thousand years later she had remained his one true and everlasting love.

He held her close to his body, feeling the warmth of her skin, smelling her rosy perfume and thinking of how he had hoped that moment would last a lifetime. However, nothing was meant to last forever for she did not know his darkest secret. And if she did, she might have to leave him. It was on that day that he saw the crone for the first time. He had not the time to dwell in his memories and had to move quickly if he wished to find answers.

It might take him months to locate the hag but he knew that she was the only one with the answers he sought. To take Reed there would endanger him but he wouldn't admit that he cared. He was done caring. He had to find Mama Jinguala then kill Jonathan and the bitch-witch.

"Take care, Reed." He growled as he took his pants off and morphed into the beast.

The Jade Necklace

Chapter Twenty: Older and Far Away

That very night, Erick was all alone in his apartment but Clara was watching. She didn't want to, but when she closed her eyes, she found herself wandering there. As usual, she could not get out, she could not break free. She was drawn to him like a moth to a flame.

He woke up late at night to a knock on the door. She assumed that it must have been Andrew who had forgotten his keys yet again. Erick grumpily walked towards the door. When he opened, they were both surprised to see that it was Grace-Marie standing before him with tear filled eyes.

"What's wrong?" he asked.

"Please, I don't want Andrew to hear."

"He's not here. Come in," he said, stepping away from the door. They sat next to one another on the old couch and he held her in his arms trying to ease her pain.

"What is it?" He asked, as Clara began to imagine the scenario that would unravel Grace-Marie had come to pretend that she realized what a great mistake it was to leave him and wanted to tell him that. She was going to beg him to take her back because he was her "one true love". He was the only man to ever put her needs above his, to give her his all, and she realized how incomplete she was without him.

But the truth was the truth… and the truth was that Erick was the only person who could put up with her drama; or so Clara thought. If this were to happen, if she were to offer herself for the taking, again, Erick would not give in too easily for she needed to learn her lesson. Otherwise she'd surely repeat the same mistakes. He would make her chase after him a few more times before he would give her his heart again. He wanted Gracie and loved her and Clara knew then and there that she had no chance with him. She hadn't seen him in person for months, not even during the training sessions. They had both been heading to the mansion at different times to train with Jacob and everyone at university could tell that there was tension between the two as they avoided being in the same place at once. He hadn't forgiven her for spying on him, but it wasn't like she had any control over her abilities.

"I... you're the last person I should be saying this to... I ... I just feel like I have no one to talk to and..." She said as he wept in his arms.

"You can tell me anything," he whispered in her ear.

"He's been ignoring me. He's not answering my calls. He's just disappeared off the face of the earth." She said as he felt a cold stab of disgust run through him, Clara was certain. *This bimbo had time to meet someone new? It hasn't been four months since the break up!*

"I..." He muttered. Gracie was there to complain to Erick about some other guy. The audacity was almost unbelievable, and Clara wished she could strangle her to death.

"Why doesn't he like me?" She cried as Erick held her tightly.

"Screw him!" he said. "That boy is blind... he's just a ..."

Clara couldn't for the life of her understand what Erick was doing. Gracie had broken up with him and she'd already moved on to someone else! She had come to complain about her new boyfriend to him. It was then that it hit her: love was blind. The same pathetic behavior that Erick displayed with Grace-Marie, was the same she displayed towards him. She was even more pathetic because the boy's heart was taken.

"How do I fix it? I don't know what to do. Should I keep on calling him?" She asked.

"Gracie, no... if he doesn't answer the first few times and doesn't call back it means he doesn't want to talk to you anymore. He was just a player, you..." he continued.

"What do you know? You don't even know him! How dare you say that about him?!" She yelled.

"Because he is... he led you on and... I hate it when you...." he tried to argue.

"This sucks... I bet you're happy that I'm feeling this bad, that I'm feeling so unwanted, so ugly, fat and... I'm all alone moping over some guy and it makes you happy doesn't it?" she yelled, finding her feet.

"What the hell are you talking about Gracie?" he yelled back. *Just slap her!*

"I just can't handle this anymore! It's too much! I'm leaving!" She said, making her way towards the door. He stopped her, grabbing her arm and forcing her body to turn towards his. It was as though their bodies were doing the Tango, the dance of fiery passion.

"Can't handle what?" he wondered, beginning to lose his temper

"You! Why are you my friend? Why do you still check up on me? Carmen and Shireen think you're acting like a stalker! That's it! It ends now..." She yelled and tried to break free of his hold.

"What does this have to do with your new boyfriend?" He asked, his grip tightening around her.

"It's just something I realized! We're done! There comes a time when two people need to part ways and this is our time! We're not fucking anymore, we're not..." she elaborated.

"Fucking?" he asked.

"Was it something more? The only reason we were doing it is because of your rock hard abs..." she replied knowing how hurt he would be. *They were fucking?* Clara realized that Grace-Marie broke up with Erick and broke his heart, but kept him around for sex like a ring wrapped around her finger and he let her to. He let her screw him over. She dated other guys and came back to his bed every night wanting more. She wanted to have her cake and eat it too. She wanted Erick in her life but wanted to sleep with other guys at the same time. She was a player.

"Is that what you've been telling people?" he asked, his voice shuddering.

"No one even knows about that," she replied.

"Gee, maybe that's why they think I'm a stalker!"

"Get out of my way... I never want to see you anymore... I don't want to be your friend! Get it?" she yelled. "Get out of my way or I'll scream!"

He finally released her. She made it to the door and stormed out almost pulling it off its hinges as it slammed shut.

Clara was torn to pieces and she hoped this was the limit. Erick was the one who had to draw the line for Marie otherwise she would feed off his soul till there was nothing left. She already knew how much he loved her, but that didn't stop her from hurting him. That girl had no conscience. *How could anyone do that to someone who loves them?* She took him for granted knowing that whenever she would cry out, he would be at her beck and call. Clara believed that it was somehow his fault for he kept on treating her well. He was definitely mistaken to still sleep with her while she saw other guys. An open relationship might have been a simpler solution for both but Erick would never want that.

Erick was too damaged to be Clara's true love. He had his own demons to fight much like she did. True love was like lasagna: sinful red comes together with serene white to form a mixture beyond words. Erick wasn't capable of that with her and she had to move forward with her life. She still had to make their friendship work somehow but she was done being his pathetic stalker, love's wretched slave. She was a grown woman, an adult, and had to start behaving as such.

****

The following day, Clara, Andrew and Widad had gathered for a small lunch at Widad's favorite restaurant: Khan el Wared.

"He punched the wall because Gracie's friends think he's a stalker," Andrew said bluntly. "I mean, who stays friends with an ex, sleeps with her and watches her date other guys? He talks about her all the time and complains about how she treats him but he isn't cutting her out! I think you need to make up with him already, Clara. He needs you."

Clara believed that his words were true but thought it insensitive to say them in such a way. She knew however, that being friends with Erick again was impossible after the situation they were both in. She might have not been able to control it but deep down she wanted to spy on him. Had she not wanted it, she could have tried harder to break free of the sway astral projection held on her. She could have tried to look away, to fly away. She could have avoided this, but on some level, she wanted to spy on him.

Erick loved Grace in spite of everything she did to him. He adored and worshiped her even though she's done nothing but harm him. Maybe that's love: pain.

Did Erick not love Clara because she was nice to him? *Didn't I attempt to get over him yesterday?*

However, what bothered her the most in that moment was her realization that Erick had led her on too at some point. Was she his plan B? Why else would he say the gentle words he spoke whenever they were alone, give her the flirty looks, give off sexual tension vibes and dance with her intimately at every party? Why else would he state how compatible they were? Why would he tell her that he loved her? Why would he tell her he wished he had dated her instead of Grace-Marie or, at least, wished that Gracie could be more like her? Was it all a game to make sure she'd be available when needed? There was no time to think of that anymore. She had moved on and wasn't planning on going back. *Supposedly.*

"I think we should stage an intervention and say: You're obsessed with Gracie. Gracie is using you whenever she's lonely and unwanted by other men, and you're letting her get away with it. We all think that way..." Widad put in.

"He will get mad," Clara interrupted.

Chapter Twenty-One:

Mama Jinguala

He could hear the rattling of chains. He had come to the right place. The dark and dank corridor reeked of death and light had no place in her kingdom. Bader could always find his way in the dark for his eyesight was akin to that of a predator. He steadied onwards through the darkness of the narrow passage knowing she would be waiting at the end. He spent months looking for her, four months to be exact and he had finally found her lair.

Mama Jinguala they called her and he had crossed paths with her before, long ago when he was Robin. It was a hot summer day when Robin and his princess were swimming in a secret freshwater lake near the castle. It had become their own paradise, shielded by large trees from the outside world; they imagined that no one knew of its existence except the two of them. He dove into the fresh water and emerged carrying her on his shoulder. She screamed and laughed and fought him. She kicked him in the face and fell in. As she surfaced, she splashed around frantically and he shielded his face by submerging himself, then reemerging between her arms planting a sweet kiss on her red lips.

"I love you, Robin."

"How sweet…" The shivering voice of an old woman sounded out of nowhere. He looked around and saw a hag standing on the soil covered in black from head to toe, a crooked nose, pale lips, and yellow eyes to see.

"Who are you?" Aurora spoke softly as she swam to the land, followed by her lover.

"My name is Mama Jinguala and I need to speak to your prince."

"I'm not a prince," Robin replied.

"And you never will be," she said just as Aurora set foot on land.

"Go to sleep child." Mama Jingula spoke and Aurora instantly fell to the ground.

"What did you do?" Robin charged at the old woman but she disappeared in a puff of smoke only to reappear behind him.

"She's just going to sleep whilst you and I have a chat. Now, sit."

He found himself forced to sit on the ground.

"I am here to offer guidance. You have a long life full of suffering ahead of you, my sweet Robin, and I am here to tell you why. Better yet, ask Agnes who your real father is."

"Caleb, Lord of the gargoyles and..."

"Then how come you don't turn to stone?" he paused for a moment. His father was Caleb and his mother the Lady Afra. Agnes took him and ran when he was five, when their castle was under attack by the very humans they swore to protect. She saved him from Lord Alaric and his men and promised to raise him until his family would one day find him. She asked him to keep his identity secret from all, including the gargoyles that protected Aurora's castle. He was taught how to suppress his other form during the night by remaining calm and not succumbing to any rage or anger. Could all this have been a lie?

"I know what you're thinking. But ask her why you had to run."

"Why are you doing this?"

"Because I need the beast that is dormant within you. I need you to reconnect with him."

"What for?"

"Lord Caleb is waging a war and you are the key to saving us all, we shall speak again after you've spoken to Agnes. Come back here tomorrow if you wish for your princess to survive."

"Don't you dare hurt her."

"I won't."

It was then that Aurora slowly opened her eyes, and just as Robin rushed to her side, the hag was gone.

"What happened?" She asked weakly as he carried her in his arms.

"Nothing to worry about."

She wrapped her arms around his neck and he carried her back to safety.

It had been years now, but he would always remember how powerful Mama Jinguala was and how great her abilities were. He did not know what she was but knew of the fear she instilled in all beings, living or dead. He continued down the corridor and glimpsed a flickering light from afar. He picked up his pace just as dizziness took over.

"Hello, darling." Her voice, all too familiar, seemed to echo all around the room and he suddenly found himself standing in the middle of a great dining hall. She walked down broad golden stairs at the far end of the hall and sat at the head of the table. She was as ugly and old as ever with her large mole bulging from her face. The only difference was that she went by white robes this time as opposed to black.

"Hello, Jinguala."

"You need Mama's help, don't you?" She said as she carved out a piece of chicken from right in front of her, a piece of chicken that had appeared out of thin air. "Have a seat, eat, enjoy."

"I need to find a man."

"Jonathan...Well, you're in luck. I need you to kill him."

"Great... where is he?"

"I won't say a word until you've eaten."

He reluctantly takes a seat at the other end of the table as her equal and finds that wine is magically being poured into an empty glass that suddenly appeared.

"You don't seem surprised anymore," she spoke with a mouthful. Bader sipped the wine.

"Taste," she said pointing at his glass of wine. "It is from a 2000 year old bottle, truly one of my treasures."

"What do you know about this man?"

"He is a Godly man. He thinks he has found a raison d'être, so to speak... He means to kill every phoenix in the world."

"Why?"

"God has once told his children of the second coming, the end of days. This man thinks the phoenixes will avert the end of days and stop the second coming; therefore, their very existence is in defiance to the word of God"

"He's mad."

"He is. You remember Geneva 16 years ago?"

"Yes."

"The girl you saved from the burning house..."

"Don't tell me she's a phoenix?"

"No, she's much more than that and she's in his way. If he kills the next phoenix she too could die. She cares for the phoenix, you see. You must do everything in your power to protect Clara Kfoury from this man... and kill him"

"You don't seem too concerned for the phoenix?"

"There are many others like him but Clara is unique…"

The room began to turn and turn around Bader. He suddenly lost balance and fell to the ground.

"What have you done?"

He could see her victims hung to the wall by chains, some still alive struggling to break free while others had rotted into bones. *Why couldn't I hear them before?* He now saw the room for what it truly was: a dungeon. The chicken she had carved out moments before had been a human torso and the wine that had been poured to him was blood that dripped from the throat of a man that had been hung upside down from the ceiling.

"I'm just helping you, poor lad."

He shut his eyes and found stillness. All was quiet and now cold. It was very cold. He could feel snow under him and when he opened his eyes, he found himself in a forest covered in snow where giant cedar trees had taken root and he knew they were the Cedars of Lebanon for that's where his enemy was headed.

"Find the phoenix and you'll find the girl." Her voice came to him and he saw an image of a young man, standing in the middle of a university campus under a banner that read: "University of Beirut". He knew he had to find them at the capital. He had saved this girl years ago when Mama Jinguala pointed the way and asked him to find her. And find her he did, saving her from a burning house. She hid cowardly under the bed as everything around her was destroyed by fire and smoke. He grabbed her and flew away into the night as she lost consciousness in his arms. She was a sweet little thing that he deposited outside of the hospital in Beirut, as instructed. He couldn't remember her face for he hadn't even looked at it to begin with. It was covered in snot. He never looked back after that day, never wondered what had been her fate. *Looks like I'm about to find out.*

He turned into his other form, spread his wings and took flight into the night. He was going to save her again and kill the man who forced Annabelle to grow up without a big sister. He was going to eat the heart of the man who slaughtered Darla.

The Jade Necklace

Chapter Twenty-Two: In the Beginning

With my mind's eye, I see a middle-aged man peacefully watching TV in his apartment when in a flash of thunder, Isabelle and I appear before him. I open my eyes just as he gasps and quickly stands, not knowing how to react. I chose this man for he lived alone and had no ties to the world. My visions had showed me that his wife had passed and that they'd never had children. As for his extended family, he had none. We needed a headquarters in Beirut and his small home was the most practical to obtain. Isabelle waves her wand at him and smiles.

"From now until my task is done

This house, yours shall be not

Keep out stranger from my home

Until yours I make it forevermore."

She chants and he promptly finds himself walking out of his home and never turning back.

"Allies and friends I call upon,

Heed my call in my hour of need,

Beirut is the beacon upon which,

You rely to come to me"

She speaks, but for some reason, nothing happens. Is she losing her ability to control the wand? Is her magic failing her? "We need our other allies. We can't kill Erick and Jacob alone," I say. In my visions, I saw that Georges was looking after them and I don't know if I can defeat him.

"I call upon you

Come to me now

Allies are you

Appear before me

In my hour of need

Come to me now."

She chants repetitively until suddenly, four men appear in our new apartment. The men seem to be exhausted from the trip. Jared, Ahmad, Jin, and Vladimir remain from the Lord's warriors after the gargoyle took our beloved Cyril. The six of us are one family, united under one cause and nothing will stand in our way.

"Jonathan, where are we?" Ahmad asks me.

"An apartment in Achrafieh," Isabelle replies. "Can we attack now? I'm bored." She sits on a leather couch. The living room is quite small and can barely fit all of us but it will just have to do. A siren sounds off in the distance and I close my eyes to see what was going on, with my mind's eye. There is an ambulance passing right by our building and the people in it are trying to save one life… and they feel good about themselves. I am trying to save the entire world yet I taste bitter charcoal in my mouth. The street we're on appears to be one of the oldest in town, unlike the posh neighborhoods of Achrafieh I had seen before.. The buildings were in decay and the sidewalks were full of trash in a way that would forbid any pedestrian from walking. All this will be made better after I kill the phoenixes and the Lord reaps the souls of the righteous. The Lord will come and save them from their filth. I shut my mind's eye and open my physical ones.

"I want to pay Jennifer Montgomery a visit first. Then we attack," I explain to them.

"Who's that bitch?" asks Isabelle as she spreads her legs and places each one on a different arm of the sofa. Ahmad shies away to avoid looking at the black thong she had on beneath her black short dress.

"Decency!" I shout and she obliges, joining both legs together on one arm of the sofa and resting her head on the other.

She turns her head to look at me and says: "Well, I'm decent enough now. So tell me Johnnie who's the bitch?"

"She's helping the phoenixes... I will warn her to stay out of my way. If she doesn't, you can do whatever you want to her," I explain. "Now go on, choose your rooms and rest. You are all going to need it," I command.

The four men go about exploring the large apartment. They are all vying for the biggest room. No matter, I don't need much space. I sit on a couch opposite Isabelle and shut my eyes as well.

I sometimes wonder why I am still working with such dark creatures and then I remember how it all started. Perhaps the source of my problem is rooted in my childhood. I was tortured and abused until the Brotherhood found and saved me. For a while, I was happy and I thought that to live in sin is actually not wrong at all. But I was young and stupid or, rather, young and in love!

He was my roommate at the Brotherhood's headquarters since he arrived a year after I had joined. He always acted strangely around me. We were young. I could sense that he was sorry for all the hurt and torture he had inflicted on me back in school. I had been the newest recruit to the Brotherhood for a while, before him that is, and had easily managed to make a few friends. Everyone seemed to pity me.

My journey towards the brotherhood began when my parents had found my diary in which I had written about my feelings towards men and my all-time childhood crush: Han Solo. I was savagely beaten by my father and brother to a bloody pulp and thrown out on the streets. My father didn't want a faggot living under his roof. I was told by my parents that if I were to remain in the same city, go to my school, contact any of our distant relatives or my imaginary school friends they would kill me. And the funny thing is that they wouldn't be blamed for killing a pervert. The law had many loopholes for hate crimes back then. I lived on the streets for weeks, rummaging through the garbage bins for food until a man found me, promising to show me a new world. He was one of the four elders who controlled the Brotherhood of the Dawn and had the sign of Wind. *If only he could see me now.* He took me to the Brotherhood's dormitories and showed me that I was special and destined for greatness. I was more than surprised to find Georges there a year later and assumed that he would go back to bullying me but he didn't. I could feel that he was sorry for what he had done to me in the past.

One night, I was having troubling dreams and he woke me up. As I looked at him I could tell that he was hard. I made him hard. We discovered our bodies' sexual impulses together that night and every night ever since. It wasn't a mere need of the flesh because I had come to love him. I love him still and I am certain he loves me. For a while, I thought we could be happy. But the Lord works in mysterious ways. He puts the sin in us to test our will, to see which one of us can rise above it. My desire for Georges and the other men is in my very nature, but only because the Lord seeks to test me. And to overcome it I must fight it with all of my soul, lest I lose it to the fires of hell.

... Who am I kidding? My soul is doomed regardless. I have taken lives. But perhaps, the Lord might take pity on me for I am his will on earth. And I have taken lives in his name! No, I mustn't fool myself. The Lord does not forgive murder even when done in his name. I am a doomed man but must do all I have in my power to save the rest of humanity. My family is all dead and they will not rise again until the second coming. If they learn that it was my doing, they might learn how to love me again, they might forgive me for sinning. I would suffer in hell but with the peace of mind of knowing that I have saved the entire world. I exist to destroy all phoenixes; such is the will of God.

Why is the weight of the mortal existence of a few against the eternal lives of everyone? I am His will on earth. It shall be done. And when it is done, the villains who have helped me will meet their doom as well.

I do not claim to be the most righteous man there is, but the Lord will forgive my sins when I die. He will. I am sure he will forgive my unnatural desires. He will forgive the deaths I have caused in His name. He will forgive me and take me into the light. I will be forgiven and loved by my Holy Father even though I will have to spend eternity in hell with the wicked. God loves me and will pardon me but he will cast me with the wicked, for that is the sacrifice that I am opting to make. My thoughts are in a loop and I need to regain my focus. Focus on the outcome.

My companions think that we will all be saved by the Lord, that we will all become Gods when the phoenixes are gone. That is a necessary evil, a necessary lie. I am the world's savior and God is my shepherd. I'm very confused, I think I want the Lord's forgiveness and I want to ascend to heaven but as Jesus said "Thy will be done" and I trust in my heavenly Father's will. His will is the death of Erick and Jacob and it will be done. They will die by my hand.

The Jade Necklace

Jad El Khoury

Chapter Twenty-Three:

Of Lords and Kings

The mountainous regions of Lebanon glowed in the night as though they were hives of fireflies. The city lights were far off but their beautiful colors drew him in. He flew towards Beirut - that's where he knew the Phoenix, Erick, and the young girl who cared for him were. He could smell the rain forming in the clouds and pressed on. Once he reached the city, his powerful sight allowed him to spot a quarrel in one of Beirut's street. It had begun to rain, and though it was heavy, it didn't stop him from soaring high into the sky. *Rain in May, must be strange for them.*

If he were to die facing Jonathan, would he be allowed to see Aurora again? *You are mine and I am yours until the end of time.*

Robin had thought his whole world had come to an end once when he had asked Agnes who his father was. She denied all claims that Lord Caleb was not his father. But after much persuasion, she sat him down to tell him the truth.

Before you were born, Lord Caleb had helped King Anais defeat the desert warriors and claim their gold as his own. The King had rallied his troops to war under the pretense that the desert King was a heathen who wanted to force his ways on the kingdom. He convinced his people that it was wiser to strike first and surprise the desert people and they did his bidding. But what the King truly wanted was the gold mines that the desert people controlled. A great war that would last a decade erupted and during that time, Caleb and Lord Alaric, the Lord of the castle Caleb guarded by night, fought side by side, each willing to die to save the other's life. They were brothers, you see, in every possible way, except by blood. One night, the Lady Afra came to the King. She was the daughter of a gargoyle Lord that had long been imprisoned by the desert people. Her people had been enslaved for over a century and forced to work the gold mines. They were all in shackles, except for Afra who had proven her loyalty to her liege more than once. She tired of her people's pain and became the embodiment of their cry for freedom. She agreed to work for King Anais in exchange for her people's freedom and safety.

One night, the Lady Afra, Lord Caleb, and Lord Alaric snuck into the desert people's city through a secret passageway that Afra had discovered. The three of them made it inside and opened the gates for Anais' armies to rampage through, killing every last man, woman, and child they could find. It was a bloodbath. The gargoyles were freed on one condition: they would swear fealty to the King and help keep the castles of his Lords safe. Caleb's reward was Afra's hand in marriage. Lord Alaric who had grown close with Afra was spiteful for he wanted her for himself, not as a wife but as a concubine. A human Lord could never wed a gargoyle. On her wedding night, after Lord Caleb went on the traditional gargoyle hunt, the lady came to Lord Alaric willingly and professed her love for him. They consummated their love and you were born. They kept it a secret and I was tasked with rearing you until you came of age.

Alaric loved you so much! He wished to proclaim you his son in the site of God and men. He wished to make you his one true heir but everyone knew that was impossible. A gargoyle could never govern the realms of men. Afra and Caleb had many children over the years as you know, but you were always his favorite, his first born. In my heart, I believe that to this day, he loves you still. He hasn't your blood but is always going to be your father for, after all, he loved and raised you.

One night, as Caleb and his men went hunting with the gargoyle Sidelle, the Lady Afra felt extreme jealousy. She felt that her Lord husband might betray her for a younger and more nubile gargoyle that had recently joined their clan. She was obviously wrong. Sidelle was merely respected for her skills as a huntress and had proven herself to be more than a match for the males. This made her rather unattractive, I believe. In her jealous mind, Lady Afra sought solace in the arms of the Lord Alaric that night. She did not anticipate that her husband would make it home earlier than usual and catch her in the act. Caleb flew into a rage and killed Lord Alaric and the

Lady Afra within moments of catching them together. He then urged his gargoyles to slaughter every man, woman, and child who ever lived in that castle. You and I are the only survivors. We managed to escape because an old hag came to me that night. I carried you as she bid me farewell and we disappeared in a puff of smoke and landed right outside this castle. Ever since then, we have been part of King Anais' court. And I thank God every day that Lord Caleb hasn't found us. To this day, I am grateful to that woman. She is the reason why we both live. Caleb is a very dangerous gargoyle and it is beyond my understanding why he hasn't struck King Anais yet. He hasn't been seen or heard of since he took Lord Alaric's castle. But I know he still lives and will return one day. But to what end, I do not know. I am certain that deep down he still cares for you but you represent the betrayal that Lady Afra had committed. The old hag told me that the Lady Afra revealed the truth of your parentage before she died. My greatest fear is that what the hag told is true. My greatest fear is that Lord Caleb will take out his anger on you and all those you love and forget that you are his son no matter where you come from.

Robin was surprised and did not want to believe. He knew that gargoyles and humans could never conceive with each other. If what Agnes said was true then that would either mean that he was a miracle child or that the belief he had previously had about reproduction was false. Either way, it would open up a world of possibilities for him and his princess. What Robin was unaware of was that Aurora had overheard the entire conversation. She walked into the room and their eyes met.

"When were you planning on telling me?" Her face was turning into a haze.

Water fell from the ceiling and wet his hair. Outside, the rain poured heavily and it somehow managed to find its way into the room through the leaky servant's roof. Aurora was wet as well, shaking.

"It's your fault!" She screamed at him as she turned pale as a corpse.

He suddenly opened his eyes and awoke with a gasp. He found himself naked in the middle of a puddle on a rainy street. He must have changed back into his human form and taken a fall. There were no cars, no pedestrians. He was all alone. All he could hear in the stillness was the sound of raindrops hitting the pavement. He got on his feet, morphed, and flew away again as the rain washed away his humanity. Only a monster can kill another monster.

The Jade Necklace

Chapter Twenty-Four:

Collision

Jennifer Montgomery walks on the sandy beach of Beirut. The heat is unbearable. Beads of sweat cover her face, her shirt is soaking wet and she soon comes to the realization that the city is on fire. The sand is piled with the corpses of those she knew: Georges, Jacob, Eric, and Clara. I stand there covered in blood and she sees me. I am not the same Jonathan she knew from long ago when we were both living under the protection of the Brotherhood. I am a new man, but I wish her no harm nonetheless. I begin pacing towards her slowly with a smile on my face. She tries to run, to move, to breathe but she's frozen in the moment. I reach her and jab my hand right through her chest pulling out her heart. She then disappears. She's presumably awake and knows that I will kill every single one of them. Hopefully, the warning is enough to thwart her and Georges from standing in my way.

***

A ringing phone jolts Erick into consciousness. I see him with my mind's eye and know that it is her. She is calling to warn him, to help him. They want to flee from me. I must act fast and get to him before they do. I do not want to face Georges again. I'm not strong enough. Erick quickly answers his phone. One question pops into my mind: Did I warn Jennifer to lead Georges to me? Did I wish for him to see me again? Did I wish for him to stop me? Of course not, I warned her so that she would stay away! I warned her so that she would keep Georges away. It backfired but the question is did I expect it to? More poignantly did I wish for my plan to backfire just so I could see him again? I love him still! I am weak!

"Hello?" He says in a semi sleepy voice when he hears my knock on the door. He gets out of his bed in a bad mood for he wished to sleep for a while longer. I can sense his every movement, his every thought. I can see him in there with my mind's eye. Jennifer will not make it in time to save him. The boy walks towards the door while still listening to what she had to say.

"Why what happened?" he asks as he opens the door.

"Hello, are you Erick Haddad sir?" I ask.

She hangs up the phone which means one thing and that is that she heard me and is coming here right now. I guess my warning was in vain. I will have to kill her and Georges.

I walk in as Erick backs away for he realized who I must be.

"You're him. I don't have any powers. There's nothing you can use against me."

"You're right."

My men Ahmad, Jinn, Vladimir, and Jared step inside and stand behind me.

"I can use theirs."

The boy quickly starts for his room, I let him go. He steps inside and locks the door.

"You don't know how sorry I am that I have to do this, Erick," I call out. "It really pains me that you have to die, especially since you don't even have powers yet."

Isabelle appears in the middle of the room with her glowing wand and smiles.

"Enough small talk? Let's get to work," she says.

"A door guarding my enemy

And a door shall be destroyed

For I must smite the sorcery

That lies behind this wall."

She chants as the door disappears.

"Time for you to do your job," she addresses me. I walk in on Erick who is holding a heated ironer with his hand.

"Couldn't you find a more creative weapon? Like a knife?" I ask.

"Fight me like a man." he taunts me. But I am not a man; I am a fag on the path of redemption.

"You're going to slowly put the ironer down." As I say the words, Erick lowers his weapon and I walk up to him.

"You see, I can make you do whatever I want. I'm wind"

"No, you can't." Erick instantly tries to push the ironer onto my face. "Jennifer taught me how to …" he says as he struggles to push. I am physically stronger than he is for I am drawing power from Ahmad's supernatural strength.

"Apparently, she did not teach you how to fight like the man you claim to be." I take it away from him and push the ironer onto his neck. He screams in agony. Barbecued skin floods my nostrils and I hope that the smell and screams won't take Vladimir's mind off the mission.

I then throw away the ironer and grab Erick by the hair, kicking him on the legs so he would kneel. I take out a knife so I can cut his throat. I stop when I hear a girl storm into the apartment.

"ERICK!" I stab the boy in the back and let go of him. He falls to the ground unconscious and bleeding as I turn back to look at her.

"Hello, Clara!" My men form a circle all around her. I step out of the bedroom and telekinetically trail Erick's dying body behind me.

"Let me have her, please," pleads Isabelle

"No...leave now girl" I tell Clara. "Or Isabelle here will have her way with you," I telekinetically fly Erick across the room and pin him to the wall. He bleeds out, his blood dribbling drown from the wall onto the floor.

"Let him go, NOW!" yells Clara.

"No."

She forces the bed to rise in the air and crash onto me just as Erick falls to the ground. Clara tries to make it to the room to help him up but Vladimir grabs her. She still manages to use her telekinesis to lift the sofa and make it fall on both Isabelle and Jared while Jinn morphs into a humongous dog.

Clara levitates herself and with Vladimir still grabbing on to her, she forces his head to hit the ceiling with force, taking advantage of his height. It does not affect him, however. He throws her at the feet of the dog who barks then attempts to bite her. She moves just in time, but he manages to take a chunk out of her right leg.

"STOP! You can't run. We outnumber you," I explain. "Leave, Clara. I am giving you this one chance."

"Kill her," Isabel orders when both Vladimir and Jinn growl.

"NO!" I yell. "We don't need to spill more innocent blood." I telekinetically pin her to the ceiling and prevent her from moving in any way, shape or form. Blood dribbles from where the dog's fangs dug deep and Vladimir wets his lips. The hunger must be too hard for him to resist but I have faith in him.

I telekinetically bring Erick to me and place him in the middle of the room on the ground.

"He's all yours, Isabelle."

A surge of power passes through every fiber of Clara's being and enormous amounts of electricity fly out of her fingers aimed at me. I groan in pain as I fall to the ground, losing control over her. I am completely incapacitated and all that I can do is watch.

As she breaks free, she falls onto the floor, face down. She bruises herself but instantly manages to stand up to her feet, her lip bruised and nose bloodied. She telekinetically throws Jinn and Vladimir into the bedroom and bars the way with the bed telekinetically then moves every single couch in the living room and stacks them in front of the doorway. She then looks at Ahmad, Jared and Isabelle. Ahmad's body lights up on fire just as Clara sends her incapacitating electivity onto Jared and Isabelle causing both of them to lose consciousness in an instant.

Ahmad rushes towards her completely on fire, setting the entire place aflame. She sends jolts of electricity at him but to no avail. He avoids all of them and reaches her. She manages to dodge his touch and decides to run to Erick's side. Ahmad sends jolts of fire that form a circle around both her and the unconscious Erick.

I know what she's thinking. She is trying to teleport both of them out of this mess but she can't. She doesn't have that kind of power. She can't even teleport herself.

In that moment, Jacob, the other phoenix, barges into the apartment instantly sending fire balls upon Ahmad trapping him in a floating bubble of fire that forbids him from breathing. He closes his eyes and manages to telekinetically move the fire surrounding Clara and aims it at the couches she had used to seal Vladimir and Jinn in the bedroom. Jacob hurries towards her and tries to help her up so that they can carry Erick and leave. As soon as they make it outside, the fire around Ahmad is extinguished and he falls to the ground, coughing. I close my eyes to see where they're going. I knew these two phoenixes were going to be a challenge. Jacob had escaped me at the Brotherhood's headquarters and was too strong to take on alone and Erick was guarded by an anomaly, Clara - powerful beyond words.

I watch them with my mind's eye running down the stairs. Jacob isn't that capable and his abilities are still not developed. He can only use fire in battle and has a super strength going for him but that is all. The only real threat is Clara, and she needs to be out of the way if both phoenixes are to die.

When they reach the main street they find that Jennifer Montgomery had just parked her car and they all get inside as she drives away.

"Clara, I need you to go home," Jennifer explains. "He's not after you."

"We need to get him to a hospital," Clara explains.

"We need to get you to the hospital," Jacob says as he notices the bite mark on Clara's leg.

"We can't! We have to run. We need a safe house. He's unstoppable."

"Can Georges heal us?"

"Yes... where is he?" asks Jacob.

"I didn't tell him where I was going...."

"Why?!! We need him!" yells Clara. She didn't tell him because she didn't want him to jeopardize the mission. Georges will be pissed when he finds out.

"We need to go to Clara's house in the mountains and hide," Jennifer says.

"How did you know about my house?" she wonders as Jennifer gives her a look that says "this isn't the time to ask questions."

"I'll ask Georges to meet us on the way and heal you both," she continues.

"Man he's gona be pissed…" comments Jacob.

"Better pissed than getting you killed," he silences him.

They're going to a safe haven. There will be five of them there against six of us. I like those odds but I'd rather get rid of the phoenixes one by one. To do that, all I need is bait.

The Jade Necklace

Chapter Twenty-Five: To Kill a Phoenix

I see her walk into her apartment building. A beautiful fake blonde who has done nothing wrong, but she happens to be the phoenix's lover. Grace-Marie is her name and she is the key to getting him alone and unprotected. She is the key to killing Erick Haddad. Isabelle steps into the building after her; her mission: to get the girl. I put myself in a deep trance in order to communicate the message to the boy. I know where he is, where he hides but I also know that I wouldn't want to come face to face with Georges. Sure, deep down I want to see him. But if I'm to succeed I cannot! I know this now especially after almost being defeated the day before yesterday. I risked everything to keep him from harm's way and ended up losing the phoenixes. If we're to face each other, one of us is likely to end up dead, most likely him.

It has been two days since I've faced the phoenixes and their guardians. By now Georges has surely healed Erick. They are ready to face us if we confront them. If they were to fight us as one then two phoenixes, Georges and the anomaly could take us. I need to get Erick to go somewhere of my choosing, eliminate him privately, and then do the same to Jacob. That way I would avoid another confrontation with their pack and Georges could live.

I drift into a deep trance and find myself in a dark room. It must be one of Erick's dreams. He must be sleeping.

He stands by the side of a red bed, naked, his body as perfect as a sculpture with every muscle drawn flawlessly on his hairless figure. His arms are flexed as he holds down a woman's behind. His curled biceps, contracting buttocks, and toned legs make me sigh. What wouldn't I give to take this woman's place? I feel myself stiffen. I long to run my fingers across his back and feel every muscle. This boy must live out of the gym and could have any woman he'd ever want. The girl's gentle hands reach for his back and gently caress their way down finding his gluts. Using them as an anchor, she bids him deeper into her. He moans in ecstasy as the sweat dribbles from his hair onto her back. He pulls her hair and shoves his .... I need to stop, I am too turned on to think. I walk towards him, grab his face and kiss him. The boy pulls out of her, explosively covering her butt cheeks, the bed and the walls with his sweet semen. Some of his cum finds its way onto my blouse. He steps away from me.

"What the fuck man?"

I always assumed that men who enjoyed anal sex were into other men on some level, deep down. I must have been luckily wrong. To sin with the one I am destined to kill would be unforgivable in the eyes of the Lord. I cannot sin with Erick Haddad no matter how much I want to.

The girl is now gone, she wasn't Grace Marie but a mere random girl he was fantasizing about. Perhaps I am mistaken; perhaps he doesn't love her as much as I thought. Then again, he is a man and all men have needs and imaginations.

Realization dawns on him as he retreats into a corner, his hard on still dribbling what I bet is the tastiest elixir that could ever roll over my tongue.

"IF you want to see Grace again,"

"Is this for real?" The boy places his hands over his crotch to cover it. He begins to realize that I am truly here.

"You're dreaming but this is real. If you want to see Grace Marie again, meet me at *Ramlet el Bayda* beach at midnight and come alone."

I fade away and wake up to see that Isabelle had gotten into the passenger seat. I look back and see the unconscious girl lying in the back seat of our Jeep.

"Someone's horny," she teases. She tries to grab hold of my hard on but I slap her hand away.

"The Lord was testing me... I passed... That boy is an adulterer in his thoughts. I am now certain that he deserves to die." Does he truly though?

"Good job Johnnie."

I drive off. When I loved Georges, never once had I had impure thoughts towards another man. All I ever wanted was him. Never once had I thought of being penetrated by another. He was my all, my heart, and my soul. Now things are different. The Lord has thought up a cruel way to test my purity and resolve. I experience impure thoughts at all times, towards any man.

It's more like a hunger. I am hungry for being fucked again. My love for Georges is still there but my lust for men has become an unquenchable burden. Perhaps this means that my quest to fulfill the Lord's mission is almost done. It is always darkest before dawn, they say. Tonight, the boy dies and there will be eleven left in the world. Soon there will be none and I will pass on to the next world in peace. I will be received by the angels and receive the highest honors as the Lord's right hand. I will find salvation and forgiveness for all I have done, for all my impure thoughts. I will be forgiven for those long nights making love to Georges in our small room at the headquarters. I will be forgiven for allowing the devil to manipulate me into thinking that loving him was no sin, that love knows no gender. I have a light within me and now is the time for it to surface to do God's bidding. The Lord will forgive me.... No! I am not worthy of his forgiveness, the Lord will merely thank me then cast me down with the wicked. But, every good soul, every saint, and the Lord himself will remember me as the savior of humanity for all eternity.

The Lord might be upset that we've been on hiatus for months, but after the injuries the gargoyle had inflicted on me, I needed the time to heal. We all needed time to regroup, gather our strengths, and plan any future assault on the twelve remaining phoenixes. I had prayed every day during that period and hope that the Lord will forgive this belatedness.

I park in front of our new building and close my eyes. I watch over Erick with my mind's eye to see if he would alert someone. Isabelle quivers next to me, a habit that shows her boredom with the long wait but I ignore her.

****

Erick woke up in the middle of the night. He was in a room all alone and it was absolutely dark. This was the same room he slept in on Saint Barbara's. He felt something wet in his pants. He placed his hand inside his boxer shorts and found that they were full of jizz. *Man I hate wet dreams.* He realized that his dream was real and that Gracie was in trouble. He jumped out of bed, took off his boxer shorts, cleaned his hard cock with tissues, and put on his jeans and a T-shirt. He might have had sex with that girl from Health class in his dream, but the one he loved was still Gracie and even though she had broken his heart, he had to save her.

He stepped out of the room into a long corridor, then made his way along it until he reached the living room. The living room was quite large with a large window that oversaw the terrace and that was why Jacob was standing guard there. Luckily, the other phoenix was in a deep sleep and Erick managed to steal away Jennifer's car keys off the table. He tip toed out of the salon again, and made his way out of the house. He then opened the main Iron Gate that separated the terrace from the main street. He then got into the car and drove off to his destination without bothering to shut the gate behind him again. He was going to die trying to save the woman he loves and that made him a hero.

I'm coming Gracie. I'm coming to save you.

The Jade Necklace

Chapter Twenty-Six: Cavalry

Clara woke up in the middle of the night. She never really slept, but instead kept tossing and turning for hours and had had it. She thought she could relieve Jacob of his watch duty seeing that she couldn't sleep as it was.

They had been hiding out in her summer home for two days. The wait was the hardest part. Jonathan did not strike at them nor try anything. To fight, is better than to wait aimlessly never knowing when the villain will strike. During that time, Erick, Jacob, and she trained as best they could under Georges and Jennifer's guidance. Georges was distant most of the time and she only understood why when she overheard an argument between Jennifer and him in the backyard one morning.

"Why didn't you tell me?" he had asked angrily. Clara could hear all too well even though she was in the kitchen that oversaw the large backyard and they stood at its very edge.

"Because you would've gotten us killed Georges."

"No... I think I can still get to him but I would never put anyone in danger..."

"That's what you think but I've seen what would have happened, had you been there. When push comes to shove, you would never hurt him. You still love him."

Clara assumed that Jennifer was speaking of Jonathan, that perhaps those two had been loves long ago. She could never put herself in Georges' shoes for it must hurt like hell to be enemies with the one you love most of all. She resolved to never bring it up nor tell the boys. She trusted Georges, though she didn't know him well and didn't want to add to his pain. As for things between Erick and her, they were better. Erick was still mad at her but considering the life-saving she had performed, he chose to put it behind him. He spoke to her almost as if he were her best friend again but still avoided spending time alone with her. Clara had noticed that her heart stopped beating fast when he was around, her hands stopped shivering, and that could only mean that her love for him was fading. She wasn't going to go as far as to admit being over him but she knew she was on the right track. She had forgiven him for somehow leading her on, because she knew in her heart that he probably did not intend to do such a thing and merely wanted to salvage the friendship.

She walked out of the bedroom and made her way through the long corridor. She almost went into Erick's room but then decided against it. She made it into the living room and found Jacob sleeping.

She woke him with a nudge.

"I thought you were supposed to be keeping watch."

"I'm sorry I must have dozed off... Are you looking for a heart to heart about Erick?"

She actually was but the only person she'd ever want to discuss that with was Andrew. Andrew, however, was clueless about her feelings towards Erick to begin with and was upset that his two best friends had gone on some camping trip without him, or so he thought. That was bound to put him out of the talking mood.

"What do you mean?" she realized that boys do talk and Erick must have told Jacob the story.

"Erick told me you two… he told me what happened…" she was extremely embarrassed but there was no point denying it.

"That big mouth… and I thought guys didn't gossip," she said trying to change the topic.

"We do it, we just go at it in a manly way."

"Did you give him a bro job too?"

"Hey! I don't give bro jobs… I wouldn't mind getting one though if the bro looks like you," she blushed. "You're a pig," she commented smiling.

"Anyway how'd you know to get to the apartment? Were you snooping again?" she actually was. She had been watching over Erick when she'd seen that he was in danger and it's a good thing she was. She did promise herself yet again to never do it anymore but who was she kidding. She was drawn to him and it saved his life.

"Kind of…"

"If you want to make up with him, I think the best thing to do is to stop snooping... friends don't watch other friends jerk off," said Jacob passing a hand through his dirty blonde hair. It had fallen all over his forehead and no longer spiked atop his head like a cockscomb.

"I didn't watch him jer...Grr! You're sick"

Jacob grinned and peeped outside.

"The car's gone..." The grin had all but disappeared and worry had crept over his face.

How could the car be gone? Who could've taken it? Clara and Jacob promptly checked the bedrooms and found that the only person missing was Erick.

****

A few minutes later, Clara, Jacob, Georges, and Jennifer gathered in the living room to discuss what could have happened. Erick was gone. Could he have left to protect them?

"Can you sense him?" asked Jacob.

"We'll try won't we Clara?" Spoke Professor Montgomery with utmost serenity.

"Yes, of course."

Clara and Professor Montgomery were going to try and use their combined ability to figure out where Erick had gone. He was in grave danger and they needed to act fast in order to save him. He couldn't protect himself, he had no active powers! Were he to face Jonathan alone, he would probably win since Jonathan could only access the powers of those around him. However, the villain had many henchmen working for him, each more formidable than the other and their powers were his to use as he saw fit.

They sat in the middle of the living room in the lotus position. They had moved the table to the side. Jacob sat on the table while Georges took to the couch. Clara took Professor Montgomery's hands in hers.

The two women closed their eyes and within moments Clara found herself floating in the ether. She was surrounded by the most beautiful of colors, colors she never knew existed and couldn't help but smile. The figure of a woman with a bright light shining from her floated towards Clara. Clara could not discern the woman's features but her eye caught the jade necklace that she wore around her neck.

"My Robin will come for you."

A large black winged beast, three times the size of the one she'd seen in her dreams, flew down from the fiery sun that reigned above them and bit deep into the woman's bosom. She screamed in pain and Clara knew that the woman was lost. A hand patted her shoulder and when she turned, she saw a man with no face, clad in black.

"You're an abomination," he told her just as he buried his fist deep into her chest. Clara gasped for air and wriggled to break free but as soon as he pulled her heart out of her chest, she found herself spiraling upwards towards the blinding sun.

She closed her eyes and found herself floating above Ramlet el Bayda beach where the sea was boiling. It was then that she awoke. She found herself drenched in sweat, on the living room floor struggling to break free from Jacob's hold.

"It's okay, It's okay..." he kept calling out to her and she calmed down. Her arm hurt and when she looked at it she saw that it was bruised. She had bumped it into something as she reacted in terror to the dream.

"Did you find him?" asked Jennifer.

"Yeah…" replied an out of breath Clara. "We don't have much time."

Chapter Twenty-Seven:

For Love

Erick steps out of his car. He steps onto the sidewalk and makes his way to the fence. He looks at the black ocean. The waves are breaking on the fence and a storm is brewing on the horizon. He feels the winds rising and buttons up his orange jacket. He covers his ears with the hood and waits. It's cold in summer and that could only mean one thing: something dark is coming.

I watch him from the car: such a beautiful young man. The area where I had asked him to meet me consisted of a long broad sidewalk, separated from the sea by a fence. It was empty that night, the cold had probably deterred anyone from heading out. I look at the gorgeous Adonis and realize that he knows he wasn't strong enough to fight me off. The boy knew what he was getting into. He came to die but wanted his girlfriend safe. Safe she will be when all is said and done. I will not bring death to an innocent. Perhaps I ought to kill him but spare his soul. That boy isn't so bad and he could deserve heaven after purgatory. No! He is a phoenix and unless their spirit is destroyed, they could be reborn and then the Lord would never return.

"Erick!" Her voice is full of fear as it calls to him. The six of us step out of our cars and start towards him. He turns around and sees her: her shirt is torn, a semi-healed scar crowns her forehead and her eyes are red and swollen with tears. Jinn, holds her forcibly. I stand in front of my five companions and step forward.

Erick takes a step towards Gracie: "Let her go."

"When you're dead baby," says Isabelle in her devilish tone.

"Isabelle!"

She smiles wickedly and walks toward Erick. She circles him.

"He's hot... no wonder you got off to those fantasies."

"Isabelle..." I command her. "Jinn let her go, he won't fight this,"

"Very well... go little girl."

Jinn lets go of Grace and she runs towards Erick. She holds on to him tightly and he drowns in her swollen eyes. He looks at her the same way Georges once looked at me.

"Erick... what's happening? Who are these people?"

"I love you."

"I love you too."

We wait. I plan to allow him ample time to say goodbye. This was the last time the boy was to set eyes on his lover. I, more than anyone, could understand the importance of these final moments. True love was always my weak spot, somehow. He did not alert anyone and it was the middle of the night. They wouldn't notice if he was missing, although, it wouldn't hurt to check. I close my eyes and my spirit soars. I see Georges driving extremely fast, with Clara and Jacob as his passengers. I love him more than anything and need to dispose of the boy before he gets here. I need to dispose of the boy before I find myself forced to kill my lover.

My eyes reopen. The boy ceases the moment, grabs his ex and kisses her fully on the lips. He tastes her sweet tongue for the last time, holds on tightly to her lower back as her hands circle his neck

"I love you," she whispers tearfully. I wish it didn't have to come to this. I did not ask for this burden but it was imposed on me nonetheless. I must not waver in my duties and must not delay.

He wipes the tears off her face and kisses her pink cheek. He then holds onto her hand tightly, nods and they both run into the night. I exchange glances with Vladimir and with a moment, he appears before them blocking their path. They are no match for a vampire's speed.

"Try to outrun me," he smiles showing them his sharp canines. Gracie screams and holds on to Erick's arm. The boy will not risk her life, he will sacrifice himself to guarantee her safety.

"Leave him if you want to live." I affirm. "Leave now girl, no one is stopping you" Gracie looks at Vladimir's teeth and looks back at Erick. She wouldn't let go of him would she? He was practically willing to die for her. She must surely want to save him as well. Alas, I had looked into that girl's heart and she didn't love him as much as he loved her. I truly wanted to spare him this discovery but looks like he's going to go down the hard way.

"I'm sorry," she cries out and tries to run across the street in a panic. She barely makes a run for it when a speeding car flips her into the air. She lands right behind it, on her face, snapping her body in half. The car speeds away into the night. Erick rushes towards his lover, his heart beating a thousand times in less than a split second. Vladimir stops him effortlessly before he reaches her. He tries to fight him off but he is no match for the vampire.

"LET ME GO!!! GRACIE!!!" he cries out in tears, but Grace Marie does not move. She remains motionless on the street and a pool of blood forms beside her motionless body. She was broken, her body was twisted grotesquely, her head and torso close to her legs, bones sticking out and blood filling a hole in the asphalt. The vampire drags Erick to my side in mere seconds and throws him at my feet. Erick raises his eyes and searches for Gracie. He looks at her broken body and realizes that she has less than a few seconds to live. The girl is still breathing, her eyes attempt to find Erick but she is lost in the darkness. Within moments, Vladimir is upon her and digs his fangs deep into her neck, drinking his fill of her blood. He was a vampire after all and could not fight his instincts.

"GRACIE!!!!!" Erick tries to get up but Jinn kicks him down.

"Enough!" Isabelle claps her hands and the ancient wand appears in her right one.

"Time to play," she smiles wickedly. Erick remains frozen, having lost the will to live. I knew that the boy felt all hope and desire to live drain out of him as he felt Gracie's soul leave her body. He is too blinded by his tears, his sense of loss. He probably doesn't feel the knife that pierced him between the shoulder blades until it was too late. He gasps in agony, unable to catch his breath. Soon he will be reunited with his loved one. There is a sense of poetic justice in this. I am doing him a favor, I am reuniting him with his princess. Not really, since his soul will perish but he doesn't know that. All he knows is that the pain that he feels will heal in oblivion. I am saving him from having to live a loveless life like the one I had. This is a mercy killing.

Isabelle's wand begins to glow and Erick closes his eyes awaiting his final fate. One phoenix down, eleven to go.

The Jade Necklace

Chapter Twenty-Eight:

Kill Jonnie

The gargoyle flew over the city. He was heading to a place called Ramlet el Bayda. Mama Jinguala had come to him in a dream. She told him where he had to go, where he would find the man he hunts for. He did not trust the crone, he never did, but surely she wouldn't lie about this. She wanted him to stop Jonathan from hurting Clara and, therefore, couldn't possibly have lied. If she did, his wrath towards her would be of unspeakable measures. He knew he could never hurt her; she was immortal and invincible but part of her power lied in recruiting others such as himself.

Years ago, after he had spoken to Agnes, he went back to see the hag by the lake. She assured him that all that was told to him was true. Lord Alaric was his father and Lord Caleb had planned a war on humanity to retaliate. He hated all men and wished for the gargoyle race to reign supremely over the earth. A good leader had seemingly changed, over-night, into a monster over a betrayal. Robin was certain that there was more to the story. He was sure that his father still loved him on some level and couldn't help but wonder what made Caleb go into remission. Mama Jinguala refused to explain the reasons why it took Caleb so long to strike but she did inform him that trouble was brewing on the horizon. Caleb had begun waging his war. He had a large army of gargoyles that hid out on one of the highest mountain peaks. That army was ten thousand strong warriors who had abandoned their respective castles. It was then that he realized that the King's guardian gargoyles hadn't been seen in weeks. Caleb was a charismatic leader and he rallied all gargoyles to his cause, claiming that they were the superior race. Mama Jinguala wanted Robin to fly off into the distance, reach the mountain caves and destroy the army while they'd slumber during the day. That was the only way to save Aurora from the horrors to come. If only he had succeeded, many of the tragedies that had shaped his life would have been averted and Aurora would have been his to love and cherish for as long as she had lived. He was going to start listening and that was why he flew to Ramlet el Bayda to avenge Darla, destroy Jonathan and save the little girl from Geneva.

He saw the sea and the seven people who stood on the pier. The exsanguinated body of a young woman lay in the middle of the street. A young man was surrounded by four walls each made of one of the four basic elements: fire, water, wind, and earth.

That's how they killed Darla.

He dove down from the sky and grabbed the witch with his hind claws throwing her into the sea. She went down screaming and the walls around the young man disintegrated. She fell into the water and narrowly avoided the rocks.

"Take him," said Jonathan.

Bader knew that the man's power came from those around him and he had to take them out in order to defeat him. A fire ball was thrown at him but he managed to dodge it and flew into the highest heights then went down like a bullet piercing the Arab's neck with his claws. The man bled out and fell to the ground. The Russian vampire jumped on Bader's back in that instant and took a big chunk out of his neck. The witch emerged soaking wet out of the water.

"He's mine!" she shrieked just as Bader tossed the vampire onto her and they both fell to the ground. She was crushed beneath the weight of his body but he knew that wasn't enough to kill her.

A car parked by the pier and the bald douche bag from the Brotherhood stepped out with the younger man who had captured him before. From the back seat emerged a young woman and with her, a volt of energy shot from Bader's heart into every fiber of his being. Time stood still for what seemed to be a century.

He knew her small pink nose, her jade eyes, her thin lips, he knew her slender physique, her heart.

He knew her!

The only thing that had changed was her hair: instead of being golden and fair, it was black as coal.

There was no mistake... she was Aurora returned to him.

He basked in the sight of the woman he loved, the woman he was denied for a millennia, the woman he had lost all those years ago and could not believe his eyes. Tears welled up in his eyes and for a moment he forgot all about the battle, he forgot all about what he had come here to do and all about the man he had wished to kill. He was looking at Aurora! It was Aurora! But how?!? How could this be? Aurora was long gone; he knew her over a thousand years ago. His heart was racing, his palms were sweating and he became a man again, weakened by his own humanity. She was his only weakness, the key to his soul. He couldn't be the beast that could defeat Jonathan when she was around. He couldn't be the beast he had become when he lost her. He saw recognition in her eyes as she slowed her pace and lagged behind her companions. She stood still and looked deep into his eyes. Does she remember me?

He was given no time to process what he had seen since Jonathan and the Asian man suddenly turned into large dragons. The Russian vampire stood next to them ready to charge as did the two witches one male, one female. They were all ready to fight. The young man they had attacked before lay motionless on the floor.

"ERICK!" screamed Aurora as she ran towards the young man but was held back by the bald douche bag. Bader realized that the young victim must have been the phoenix, Erick, who would cost the girl he was sent to protect, her life. However, could Aurora be the same Clara he was sent to protect? She did not seem to recognize him and it was very much possible that she had forgotten their shared history.

No... the look in her eyes at first glance said it all. Her soul recognized his own at some level, he was sure.

"Powers of all earth and stars

Take away all that she is

Strip her from all her strength

Or that girl will never live."

The witch chanted as her wand glowed and sent an energy beam straight at Aurora.

She may not remember him but he had to save her. He could not allow her to die. He morphed back into a beast flew towards her. She was hit by the bright light that emanated from the wand. As she was falling to the ground, he grabbed her and flew off into the stars. He would forgo revenge if it meant that she would survive. He would forgo revenge for love.

"Let me go!" she kicked and screamed as they levitated into the air. One of the dragons, the Asian, was on their trail, however, whilst the other engaged in combat with the men who had accompanied his princess. The dragon was too fast. He caught up with them and breathed fire, hitting Bader fully on the back forcing him to drop her. She screamed as she fell spiraling to the ground. He dove after her but the dragon grabbed him with its claws piercing his back. Bader growled at him, accelerated his speed to free himself and flew upwards jumping on the dragon's back and as the dragon breathed out his flames, he managed to grab his jaw with both of his arms and broke it. The dragon changed back into the corpse of the Asian man and fell out of the sky. His

Aurora was still tumbling towards the ground screaming: he was about to lose her again and that was something he wasn't going to allow. Not again. He sped towards her with all his might and managed to grab her at the last second. The moment he held on to her, she stopped screaming. He rose again into the sky, his gaze lost in hers. She did not look at him through the eyes of love but she wasn't afraid anymore either. The jade necklace that was tucked away beneath her white blouse now glistened around her neck. It was the same necklace and that was all the proof he needed to know that it was her. She looked like an exact replica of his love and wore the same necklace she had worn a thousand years ago. This was Aurora even if she did not remember. She eyed him with wonder, possibly trying to grasp who her savior was. She could be trying to remember why all this seemed all too familiar, her heart could be remembering that she loved him once before.

"Put me down!" he complied and put her down on an empty rooftop. She immediately ran towards the exit but he grabbed her by the arm and stopped her. She wanted to go back to the beach, to try and save Erick. He was not going to allow her to face any more danger.

He would save Erick for her and get the revenge he sought but she had to stay safe. He turned into a man. He wasn't sure whether he wanted her to remember him. He had no idea how he was going to explain how much he'd changed since last they'd been together. She shied away from looking at his member and blushed. As innocent as ever. For the first time in forever, he was self-aware. A tear formed at the corner of his eye and slowly drew a path on his cheek.

"Who are ... You?" she asked.

He could sense that she might have remembered something. Was she truly Aurora? Was she his princess? Or was she the product of a genetic pool of luck? She is Aurora and that is Aurora's necklace.

"I know you... you were there! You were there in Geneva! You saved me! You know what happened to them! To my parents! You ...!"

The little girl Mama Jinguala sent me after. This was Clara, there was no doubt. She was the girl the old crone had sent him to keep safe. Was she special because her soul was older than time? When he saved her, it hadn't occurred to him, she was young and he was furiously trying to keep her safe. He never would have thought that the little girl he rescued in Geneva would have been his princess, or her reincarnation or her genetic clone. He never would have imagined it. He was certain that he was looking at the soul of the only woman he ever loved.

"I want answers!" *The bratty attitude is new.*

"I have none," he said coldly. He wanted to hold her in his arms again more than anything in the world. He wanted to kiss her, to make her feel safe, to protect her. But first, he needed his revenge. He wasn't ready to forget about Darla and what Jonathan did to her. That man would hurt Aurora too if he wasn't stopped. Mama Jinguala had sent him to protect her as a child for a reason. She wasn't a phoenix, true, but apparently she was much more than that and once that wicked bastard were to realize what she was, he would surely make an attempt for her life. As long as she was away from the battle, he was ready to go back and fight Jonathan and his witch. As long as Aurora was safe, vengeance was his.

"Stay here, don't move," he said as he morphed into a beast. She grabbed his curled arm with her soft gentle hands.

"Take me with you."

"No."

"You bastard!" she yelled. "You asshole!" She punched at him with all the might of a fly. "You took me from that house in Geneva and you let them die! You let my family die! You left them to burn! And you placed me in... I grew up... I thought I was... You left me to think I was insane! And scarred and..."As she continued to yell and punch at him, he gave her his back and readied himself to soar. He had not seen any family members when he broke into her room as a child and had he, he would have surely saved them. He had no time to explain himself at the moment.

"Don't you walk away from me! You took my family! You're not going to take Erick too!" He took off and flew into the night's sky ignoring her pleas.

"I will kill you if anything happens to him! You hear me?!"

The Jade Necklace

I love you! Many questions ran through his head and he planned on getting answers. But first, he had a monster to slay.

Chapter Twenty-Nine:

The Last Stand

Georges steps out of his car along with that girl, Clara, and the phoenix, Jacob. They've come earlier than anticipated. No matter, two birds with one stone is not a bad deal. Erick is almost dead and his death will put off Clara. She would lose the will to fight. Georges isn't willful enough to take me and that leaves out Jacob. I can take him.

I turn into a dragon. If Georges is to die at my hand, I'd rather spare him the realization that I am truly lost to him as he looks into my eyes before releasing his soul into the hands of the angels, or demons. I'd rather kill him in dragon form. That way, he could console himself into thinking that I was not myself.

Jinn turns into a dragon as well, while Isabelle, Vladimir, and Jared stand strong beside me. It is in that moment, that the gargoyle turns back into a man. This is our chance. The girl is new to her power, one phoenix is defenseless and bleeding out, the other can barely access some abilities and Georges is weak. Bader, however, shifts back to his beastly form and flies towards the girl and takes her out of the game, both of them flying away. Jinn takes off after them in order to finish off this nuisance of a gargoyle that has been hunting for us. It is up to the rest of us to take out Georges and his phoenix.

"Give up old man," says Isabelle. It is then that Jacob sends multiple fire bolts at her but she manages to thwart them. Jared was not as lucky and found himself set ablaze. The screaming man tries to extinguish the flames off by rolling on the ground but Jacob's resolve is stronger than ever and with a twist of his hand, he snaps Jared's neck. It is quite impressive how he is coming into his new powers. He could very much be the phoenix from the prophecy.

"You're a big boy now." she says. "Let's see you handle a dragon…" I strike at him and attempt to take a chunk out of him but he rolls under me and manages to avoid my fangs. Georges turns into a dragon as well to defend his protégée. It has come down to this: two lovers fighting to the death and the fate of the world hanging in the balance. It is rather poetic. He strikes at me with his tail and sends me crashing into an electrical pole. I look at Isabelle and she understands what she and Vladimir must do. Vlad rushes at Jacob and kicks him down. Jacob manages to thwart him and jumps on my back. I take off into the air and fly with my back down and shake him off. The boy falls down and is caught by Georges. Georges attempts to fly away but I descend on him with my claws and pierce his hind. Jacob falls down and, as Georges growls in agony, he manages to catch him with his tail. I dig my claws deeper into his skin and the man that I love bleeds out and is forced to let go of his phoenix. Jacob falls to the ground breaking his leg. His femoral bone breaks in two and pierces his skin sticks out. The boy screams in agony. Vladimir, smelling the blood, rushes towards the phoenix. Georges attempts to get me off but I don't oblige. I bite his neck and taste his metallic blood and the memories flood my being. I let go and he falls to the ground.

I remember our first kiss in our dorm room, the first time his eyes told me that he had bullied me at school merely because he saw something in me that he was afraid to admit about himself. I remember the first time he told me he loved me when we were 17 walking down the cold streets on Christmas Eve. I remember the last night we spent together when I had told him of my quest to do God's will. I remember how I broke his heart then and realize that now I have broken his body. Georges crashes into the ground and turns back into a bleeding man who is barely capable of standing up. I land beside him and change back. Vladimir reaches Jacob who attempts to crawl away.

"Where do you think you're going little man?" The vampire licks his wound and smiles. "You taste like chicken…"

"Vladimir… let him be…. Isabelle do your work." I take a knife from Ahmad's body and walk to the boy. Georges and I are both naked, the pieces of cloth that remained from our clothes barely fixed on our bodies from the shape-shifting. This makes things a little more interesting: two lovers fighting as God intended, one on the side of the angels, the other on the side of the devils.

"Jonny don't …. Please," cries out Georges in agony. I hesitate. I serve God and only God and this is my final test.

In that moment, the gargoyle returns. Jinn must have failed. He lands right in front of me and kicks me across the face. I fall to the ground just as Vladimir punches him in the crotch and bites his neck again. The gargoyles growls, grabs Vladimir by the hair, and flips him onto the ground. He then lifts him up in the air from his hair, places his other hand on his shoulder and decapitates him by pulling hard. My companion turns to dust and crumbles right before my eyes. Vladimir was the only one who knew of my real purpose and that was why I had Isabelle imbue his daylight necklace with the souls of countless other vampires to make him more powerful than the average creature of the night, more powerful than other pure bloods even! If Bader could kill him with ease then I had cause for alarm. Isabelle appears to be frightened for the first time and takes a step back. She raises her wand in his face as I get back up on my feet.

"Try it and lose an arm…" Bader says.

"Powers of darkness I summon thee…" she begins to chant as he speeds towards her, breaks her arm, takes the wand out of her hand and breaks it in two.

"NOOOOOO!" she cries out. He grabs her by the neck and lifts her off the ground just as I send my flames at him and he is forced to let her go. She runs off into the night as I make the flames take the form of a sphere that surrounds him and consumes the oxygen around him. He struggles and tries to break free but cannot. The oxygen begins to thin around him and he begins to drift into unconsciousness that will soon become sweet death. I smile. I might not be able to destroy the phoenixes' souls without Isabelle but at least they'll be gone long enough for God's plan to take shape. They have to pay the price of the world's salvation.

Everything I have done throughout my life has lead me to this moment. It has lead me to save humanity by sacrificing the soul of the few for the benefits of the many. I am willing to sacrifice my soul for that glorified mission. I am willing to sacrifice Georges and everyone I have ever loved if that is what it takes to save the world.

I feel a cold sharpness pierce my back and I gasp losing my hold on the gargoyle who falls still to the ground. I turn around and see the bleeding Georges standing behind me with his hand clutched at the knife he used to stab me in the back.

"I'm sorry," he says as I fall to the ground barely able to breathe or utter any words. He kneels beside me and takes me in his arms. I look around me and see that both phoenixes and the gargoyle are unconscious or dead and know that my mission must have been completed. Though there are more phoenixes, the majority has been eradicated at my hand and the Lord will surely choose another to take my place. I smile at my Georges as he holds me close to his chest in tears.

"I love you," he says to me. I see us walking down that street in coats, gloves, and winter shoes, hand in hand on the deep snow. I see him take off his glove and touch my face with his freezing bare hand in the middle of the street... right there in the middle of it for everyone to see. His hand was freezing but it emanated warmth and love as he caressed my face. He whispered to me "I love you" on that day and it was like music to my ears. I had never felt so safe, so pure. I often longed to go back to that moment when I took off my own gloves and tucked my fingers in his hair before I kissed him then and there to the echoes of the OHs and Ahs of the judgmental passersby.

In this moment, I wish we could have remained like that. I wish we had never parted. I wish we had been glued to that snow, forever trapped in that moment of peace. I wish the Lord had chosen another warrior. I wish that the path to righteousness did not involve such torment and self-loathing. Perhaps to hate oneself is not the right path. What life could we have had if I had chosen him and not the path of the Lord? Maybe we'd have lived in sin, maybe we would have risked eternal damnation but at least we would have lived! Am I not a damned man either way? I am going to hell anyway couldn't I have at least enjoyed my last days with the man I love before having to spend an eternity in hell? And would it truly be a place of eternal torture and damnation if we were going there together?

"I....lo..." I struggle to speak but the places his finger on my mouth.

"I know," he reassures me.

I begin to drift into the unknown. At least, Georges survived me. He will endure and be finally free of the shackles of my love. I am free.

****

Clara reached the pier and saw Georges kneeling beside Jonathan. She saw the naked beast that tried to get her away from the carnage unconscious on the ground. He may not have harmed her family but he chose to harm her in other ways. He could have explained things to her, he could have taken her somewhere safe where she could have learned about her powers. Instead, he abandoned her like a stray dog. She did not care for his wellbeing, but wanted the creature to survive only so she could question him. Why didn't he save them? Why did he save her and her alone?! Where was her sister? She had to know and that monster was the key. Her eyes then caught Jacob who lay out cold by an electric pole with a bone sticking out of his thigh and Eric bled out on the ground a few meters away from the others.

She rushed towards Erick hoping against hope that he was still alive. She tried for his pulse and found it to be too faint.

"Can you help him?! Please help him!!"

Georges let go of the murderer's body and walked towards Clara. He kneeled beside her and laid a hand on Erick's forehead. He loved Jonathan. She recalled the conversation she had overheard. It must have been very painful for Georges to lose the one he loved. She did not dwell on those thoughts. Erick and Jacob were dying and Georges was her only hope of saving them both. They would both cry about his lost love later but now, he had to save Erick. He closed his eyes as Clara's tears rolled down her face. Georges' breathing grew heavier and heavier and he started to sweat. He appeared to be losing too much energy in the process and heavy blood poured out of his wound. This never happened before. When Georges healed her and Erick, he seemed to do it effortlessly. She wondered if the loss of Jonathan combined with the wounds he sustained in battle had an effect on his healing. It was as though he was healing Erick with what was left of his own life. A few minutes passed and the gargoyle regained consciousness. He stood up and his eyes met Clara's from a distance. That man is the only living being who had any idea, no matter how remote, about where she came from and what she was. She was angry at him for leaving her family, but it seemed like the creature had her best interest at heart. He flew her away from the battle to shield her from harm. That still didn't merit any trust nor forgiven ace for she did not know him and did not know of his motives, but she felt that he wasn't as evil as he looked. She had a million questions to ask him but could not now for Eric's life hung in the balance.

The man's hazel eyes still pierced hers from afar and she felt like the memory of him was far out of reach yet so close. Who was he? His sight rapidly shifted to the dead Jonathan. He growled, turned into a beast again, and flew off just as Erick gasped for air.

"Erick! Erick!" Clara hugged him and kissed his forehead, holding on tightly to him. Georges crawled away from them towards Jacob and placed his hand on the broken femur. Clara could still hear Georges' labored breathing through her tears of joy as Eric struggled to get off the ground.

"What happened?" he asked just as he saw Gracie's broken body and rushed towards her in tears. He ran halfway then crawled on all fours for the rest of the distance, crumbling beside her body. He dragged her towards the side-walk and held her in his arms crying.

It was in that moment that Clara knew who the holder of his heart was and always will be even in death. She was not going to be the villain of this story; she was not going to be the one who thrives off the death and pain of others. Gracie's death pained her. She had no love for the girl but never wished her this kind of harm. She wanted her out of Erick's heart but never wanted to see her dead in the middle of the road. She was now certain that Erick was not hers and will never be. She deserved better. He deserved better. After Gracie's death, she felt as though it was more forbidden to want him. It would be a betrayal to their friendship if she were to think of him that way still. Her sight shifted to Jacob and she saw him get up but next to him Georges crumbled on the ground. She made it to his side and tried to shake him but the man did not respond. She checked for a pulse and found that it was gone. Jacob, frantically, attempted CPR on his mentor as Clara stared into the void.

Georges had given his life to bring back the phoenixes. He had the power to heal but at the expense of his life energy and he gave every last drop of it to save those two boys. Perhaps he willed to die. Perhaps he chose to be reunited with Jonathan again. Everyone around her made sacrifices while she obsessed over a selfish impossible one sided romance with a friend. She needed to grow up and she needed to help that friend become who he is meant to be so that Georges' sacrifice would not be in vain. She needed to be the woman she'd always knew she could become. It was in that moment that she realized that she was free of the thrall Erick held over her. She did not smile for she had just lost a friend but she was unburdened and felt ready for what was to come. She was going to guard the phoenixes.... For Gracie and for Georges!

*****

Bader flew over Beirut for the last time. He could not confront her. That girl was Aurora. She may not remember, she may not know it, she might even hate him but she was Aurora and fate had put her in his path. He needed to understand how that could be and only one creature on earth had the answers. He was going to seek out Mama Jinguala and force her to give him straight answers once and for all.

Epilogue: The Shape of Things to Come

It rained heavily over the Atlantic Ocean.

A light glowed from beneath the water and a large whirlpool appeared. It swallowed a nearby ship. It then ejected a light beam into the sky. A glowing portal appeared right above the ocean and a black, scaled hand pulled itself out. A black, scaled body fell out of the portal into the water as it stopped spiraling.

Moments later, a dark face emerged from the water then a tall largely built figure flew into the sky. The creature looked very much like a gargoyle, only he was bigger, taller, and better built than Bader. He had coarse features, sharper fangs and teeth and seemed to be very angry.

He flew over the ocean till he saw many lights at the edge of the water. He had come into a new world. He must have been in his prison for centuries and had finally broken free with one intention in mind. He craved revenge. He needed to destroy the one beast that put him there. He was going to kill every single person that man held dear and he was going to make him watch. He was going to destroy his life and tear it apart. He was going to make him suffer for trapping him in the void and for destroying his life. He was going to make him pay a hefty price for existing.

What he wanted now was no different from what he had wanted for the past thousand years: to devour Robin's beating heart.

This had all transpired in Mama Jinguala's mind and she smiled at the vision she had just had.

Jad El Khoury

First edition published by TADROS PUBLISHING

February 2016

info@tadrospublishing.com

www.facebook.com/tadrospublishing

Twitter.com/@tadrospub

www.tadrospublishing.com

Printed in Great Britain
by Amazon.co.uk, Ltd.,
Marston Gate.